DEATH BEFORE DINNER

Kolabuk's arm was a blur as he sent the long-bladed Bowie spinning across the room. The weapon found its mark before the trapper could fire a second time. It buried itself up to the hilt in the left side of the man's buckskin jacket. The Winchester clattered to the saloon floor, and the trapper stood there, weaving on his feet for a moment, before his eyes rolled up into his head and he joined his partner in death.

All eyes watched as the Eskimo crossed to the two dead men and yanked his Bowie from the chest of his last victim. He took a lengthy swallow from the jug the two men had shared and, crouching, began to search the bodies for valuables.

Monty Boyd and Henri Gastineau turned back to their own drinking. "I knew he'd get the best of them," said Gastineau. "Kolabuk is faster than the strike of a rattler, with gun or knife. It was no contest, in my opinion."

Monty nodded in agreement, then turned back to his squaw. "Throw another steak on the griddle for Kolabuk here. Then drag these carcasses outside and scrub that mess off the wall over yonder. It's enough to ruin a man's appetite."

DON'T MISS THESE
ALL-ACTION WESTERN SERIES
FROM THE BERKLEY PUBLISHING GROUP

THE GUNSMITH by J. R. Roberts
Clint Adams was a legend among lawmen, outlaws, and ladies. They called him . . . the Gunsmith.

LONGARM by Tabor Evans
The popular long-running series about U.S. Deputy Marshal Long—his life, his loves, his fight for justice.

LONE STAR by Wesley Ellis
The blazing adventures of Jessica Starbuck and the martial arts master, Ki. Over eight million copies in print.

SLOCUM by Jake Logan
Today's longest-running action Western. John Slocum rides a deadly trail of hot blood and cold steel.

JAKE LOGAN

SLOCUM AND THE GOLD SLAVES

B

BERKLEY BOOKS, NEW YORK

SLOCUM AND THE GOLD SLAVES

A Berkley Book / published by arrangement with
the author

PRINTING HISTORY
Berkley edition / September 1994

ISBN: 0-425-14363-5

BERKLEY®
Berkley Books are published by The Berkley Publishing Group,
200 Madison Avenue, New York, New York 10016.
BERKLEY and the "B" design
are trademarks belonging to Berkley Publishing Corporation.

PRINTED IN THE UNITED STATES OF AMERICA

10 9 8 7 6 5 4 3 2 1

1

John Slocum awoke in a dimly lit room. At first, he failed to recognize his surroundings—the floral print of the wallpaper, the four-poster bed of sturdy oak, and a standing wardrobe with mirrored doors. Then he smelled the faint scent of salt in the air and heard the distant ringing of fishing buoys in the bay, and he knew.

San Francisco. He had arrived in the seaside town early that morning, amid a pea-soup fog that was so thick you could have almost cut it with a knife. Slocum had endured a long ride from Carson City and, after leaving his horse at a livery stable at the city limits, sought the comfort of a hot breakfast and a soft bed.

He had found both at the hotel he now awoke in. It was named the Langstrom House, from what he recalled. The four-story brick building had seemed inviting enough—particularly the odors of coffee and food that drifted from within—so he had gone inside. He had bought himself a breakfast of ham and eggs, grits, and big cat-head biscuits, as well as a cup or two of strong black coffee. With his belly full, Slocum had left the dining room, checked in at the front desk, then climbed three flights of stairs to his room. The hotel had one of those newfangled elevators, but Slocum had refused to ride in the iron cage. The cable that took the contraption from one floor to the next didn't look all that sturdy to him. If he was to die, Slocum was

1

determined to do it on the back of a horse or with a gun in his hand, and not by falling several stories due to some crazy fluke of bad luck.

When he had reached his room, he found that the ride from Nevada had been more exhausting that he had first thought. He drew the shade on the window, tossed his gear aside, and lay down on the bed. The soft folds of the feather mattress felt like a cloud underneath him, and before he knew it, he was fast asleep.

Now, several hours later, he sat up on the bed and yawned. The heaviness of his slumber clung to his mind and muscles, but he shrugged it off. Obviously, quite a bit of time had elapsed during his nap. The room was gloomy; only pale gray light filtered around the edges of the window shade. And his stomach growled like a hungry dog, almost painfully so. Apparently, the belly-busting breakfast of ham and eggs had long since run its course.

Slocum sat on the edge of the bed for a moment. He stretched, then stood and walked to the window. He lifted the shade and stared through the dirty panes at the city that stretched below.

The last light of day faded in the west, coloring the broad harbor of San Francisco Bay with gleaming strokes of violet and gold. Slocum could see ships on the water, as well as parked along the many docks that made up the seaport's waterfront. Most were huge steamers of wood and iron, while others were smaller fishing boats.

But the bay lay a good half mile away. Slocum shifted his gaze to the city itself. San Francisco stretched as far as the eye could see; a jumble of stone and brick buildings, many well over three stories high. The streets were lit with gas lamps, and despite the chill of the season, the sidewalks were crowded with people. Slocum laid his palm against the glass of the window. It was cold to the touch, from the low temperature of the December evening.

Slocum recalled his long ride from Nevada to the California coastline and felt thankful that he had reached San Francisco before becoming caught in a winter snowstorm. He had been stranded in blizzards before, in the Colorado Rockies and on the plains of Montana, and he had nearly frozen to death in both. That was his main reason for coming to San Francisco. He had a little money in his pockets and would prefer spending the next couple of months in some warm saloon, drinking and shuffling the pasteboards, rather than holed up in some mountain cabin or riding across some icy range with nothing between him and the north wind but open prairie.

Slocum turned away from the window. He walked to a table next to the bed and, taking a sulfur match from his vest pocket, lifted the chimney of a coal oil lamp and lit the wick. Soon, a soft glow was cast over the room and its modest furnishings. The Langstrom House wasn't the fanciest hotel in San Francisco, but neither was it the cheapest dive in the city.

His gear was right where he had left it. His boots stood next to the bed, his hat hung on one of the four oaken posts, and his saddlebags, coat, and gunbelt lay in a heap on a cedar chest next to the footboard. Slocum donned his boots, then buckled the gunbelt around his waist. His Colt Navy revolver rested in a cross-draw holster with the butt jutting across his belly, easily within reach of his right hand. After tightening the buckle, Slocum thought nothing more of the six-shooter. He had been carrying the .36-caliber pistol since the War Between the States, and over the years, it had practically become a part of him. If he needed it, he always knew where it was.

As he shrugged on his fleece-lined coat and took his hat off the bedpost, John Slocum caught a glimpse of himself in the mirror. Although it wasn't for him to say so, he was a handsome man—tall, powerfully built, with a shock of raven-black hair and striking green eyes. Whenever he spoke, he gave away the locale of his upbringing. Slocum was a Southerner, born and bred, hailing from the state of Georgia. It had been a long time since he had seen the South, with its battle-scarred countryside and rampant poverty, but the enduring spirit of Dixie went with Slocum wherever he traveled. It was simply a part of his soul.

Slipping his hat on his head, the drifter left his room and stepped into the decorative hallway. A grandfather clock at the end of the corridor told the time as being half past five in the evening. No wonder his belly was carrying on like it was. He had unwittingly slept past dinnertime. He supposed he would have to make it up to his grumbling stomach when he sat down at the supper table.

He avoided the elevator once again, choosing to take the stairs. When he reached the lobby, he found it nearly empty. The clerk stood behind his desk, depositing mail in slots along the wall, while several men sat in plush armchairs near the front window, smoking cigars and reading that day's newspaper.

Slocum crossed the lobby to the dining room. When he stepped through the doorway, he found that several people were already seated at the tables. Some were ordering their meals, while others sat and waited for theirs to be brought from the kitchen.

The Southerner was searching out a table where he could spend his time quietly, when someone yelled from across the room. "Slocum! John Slocum!"

The sound of his name being called out startled the drifter a little. Instantly, he let his hand drop to his waist, the thumb hooking over his buckle, where only a slight motion would put the Colt in his hand at a moment's notice. Few men knew the name of John Slocum, and those who did were mostly men with a grudge, or federal lawmen. Slocum had done things in his past—some that he was proud of and some that he wasn't. One or two of those things had put his name and description on wanted posters, either for the right or wrong reasons. That had been a long time ago, but a man's past could come back to haunt him when he least expected it. Slocum had learned that bitter truth several times before.

The tall Georgian's eyes narrowed as he shifted his gaze from one table to another. He found the one he was looking for next to the kitchen door. The man at the table motioned for him to come nearer, so Slocum did so, though cautiously.

Slocum didn't recognize the man at first. He was a tall, lanky fellow dressed in the dusty duds of a trailhand. His long face sported a receding hairline and a blond mustache that drooped past the point of his chin. It was when Slocum spotted the man's hat—a ten-gallon silverbelly Stetson with a single bullet hole through the peak of the crown—that he finally realized who the cowboy was.

"Tex?" he asked, easing his hand away from his gun. "Tex McCoy?"

"The one and only," said the rawboned man with a Texas drawl. "What are you standing there gawking at, John? Sit down and join me."

Slocum shed his coat and hat, then pulled up a chair and sat across from the man. He stared at the Texan and shook his head. "Well, I'll be damned. Didn't think I'd ever see you again. Especially up in this neck of the woods."

Tex McCoy laughed. "Like a duck outta water, right? Well, I'll tell you what, John. I spent the better part of forty years breathing Texas dust and cow manure, dodging mesquite thorns and rustlers' bullets. So I set out to see what lay west of the Pecos River. And I ain't slowed down since."

Slocum ordered his food from a waiter, then sat back in his chair and regarded the man across from him. The last time he had seen Tex McCoy was after a cattle drive from San Antonio to Amarillo. Along the way, Slocum had encountered rustlers, miles of waterless prairie, and even the fury of a Texas twister. He had also made a friend of Tex McCoy, even though their association with each other had been temporary. In fact, Slocum would hazard to say that McCoy was one of a choice few who knew him by his true name and not his much-used alias of Smith. He remembered Tex as being a man one could trust with a secret, or even his life, if it came down to it.

"So what are you doing here in San Francisco, Tex?" asked Slocum.

The cowboy smiled, revealing a mouthful of tobacco-stained teeth. "Well, it's like this. I was heading through the Sierras, looking for a place to stay the winter, maybe grub for my room and board. Then that wind turned mighty cold, and I could smell the snow brewing, sure as anything. So I hightailed it on up here to Frisco. Thought I'd find a few odd jobs around town and spend my spare time gambling and whoring. It's a better way to wait out the spring than to sit in some cold bunkhouse getting wild with cabin fever. What about you, John?"

"I came here for pretty much the same reason," admitted Slocum. "Haven't had much of a chance to get out yet, though. I just rode in this morning."

"You ever been in San Francisco before?"

The Southerner nodded. "A couple times, but it's been a few years."

"What do you say you and me paint the town tonight, John?" asked Tex. "I came to see the elephant, and by

God, I want to see every hair and wrinkle of the dadblamed critter. Know any good places hereabouts?"

"Several," replied Slocum. "There's the Lucky Wheel Saloon on Market Street and the Golden Dragon in Chinatown. Then there's the Union Club on Knob Hill, but I don't think you'd fit in there. Mostly a bunch of high-class dandies in ties and tails. No place for an old cowhand like you."

A sly look bloomed in Tex's blue eyes. "Well, now, I wouldn't mind playing a game or two of faro or blackjack, but what I'm really looking for don't have nothing to do with cards or dice."

Slocum nodded. "Women."

"That's right," said Tex. "Been a long spell since I've had me a city whore. What about you?"

"I wouldn't mind the company of a lady tonight," agreed the Georgian.

"Then that settles it," said McCoy. "And I know just the place. Ever since I rode into town, I've heard about this place they call the Blue Orchid. Finest bordello in San Francisco, they say. Claim that they've got fifty ways to pleasure a man. Can you imagine that? Fifty ways! Hell, I didn't know there was over five or six."

Slocum smiled to himself. He thought back to the women he had encountered in his life and the ecstasy he had shared with them. There had been many, and each had left her own lasting impression on him. So, in a way, Slocum knew that the number could go well beyond the mythical fifty that the Blue Orchid boasted.

"So, how about it, partner?" urged Tex. "How about you and me going down there and sampling what they have to offer? They say the place has gambling and whiskey, too, as well as the prettiest heifers in town."

"Where is this whorehouse?" asked Slocum.

"Down on the waterfront, near Battery Street," said Tex eagerly.

"I've been down there before," said Slocum skeptically. "It's the roughest part of town."

"Hell, what do we care?" scoffed the cowboy. "We spat in the face of Ol' Lucifer when we were on that cattle drive. A few crusty longshoremen and drunkards shouldn't give us any trouble."

Slocum thought the proposal over as the waiter brought their food—a couple of thick, juicy stakes with potatoes and buttered slabs of sourdough bread on the side. Although he had spent most of his time in the hotel eating or sleeping, he could still feel that familiar restlessness begin to surface. It was the same feeling of entrapment he felt whenever he was surrounded by a ceiling and four walls for even a short period of time. He felt the need to roam, even if his roaming was confined to the gaslit streets of San Francisco.

"All right," he finally agreed. "I'll go with you."

Tex McCoy grinned as he tucked the linen napkin in the collar of his shirt and lifted his knife and fork. "Hoo, boy, are we gonna have some fun tonight!"

"I certainly hope you're right," said Slocum. He took his own silverware in hand and went to work on the beef before him, the growl in his belly noisily urging him on.

2

An hour later, John Slocum and Tex McCoy were on the streets of San Francisco, making their way toward the waterfront.

The colorful sunset had bled away, leaving only the darkness of twilight. An evening fog rolled off the cold waters of the bay, slowly creeping through every avenue and alleyway of the seaport city. The gas lamps on their iron posts glowed hazily in the mist, but the fog hung in the air thickly, obscuring the streets at only a short distance. Soon, the pedestrians who had crowded the sidewalks before decided it would be best to seek the shelter of warm parlors or smoky saloons, depending on which social class they belonged to.

Slocum and McCoy seemed to pay the fog no mind. They strolled along Market Street, heading toward the edge of the bay. They talked as they went, reminiscing about their cattle drive across Texas, but they did not walk blindly. Their eyes constantly darted toward upcoming corners and the dark entrances of alleyways, searching for some telltale sign of danger before it could appear unexpectedly. If any menacing souls hid there, out of sight, they apparently decided to let the two pass, unhindered. Slocum kept one hand hooked in his belt, close to the Colt Navy, while McCoy's gun hand hung easily at his side, only an inch or so from a low-slung Remington forty-four.

It wasn't long before they finally reached the waterfront. The docks were even more ominous and choked with shadow than San Francisco's central streets. Stacks of wooden crates and barrels of crude oil and pickled fish stood high and thick along the boardwalk. Every so often, a rat the size of a tomcat would dart across the men's path, then disappear into the murky darkness just as swiftly. There was also the occasional glow of cigarette ash as a down-on-his-luck seaman leaned against the boarded wall of a warehouse, keeping his eyes peeled for some well-to-do drunkard that he could roll, given half the chance.

It took them a half hour of steady searching to find the place they were looking for. The Blue Orchid was not much to look at from the outside. It appeared to have been a warehouse before it had been converted into a place of vice. The only indication that it was something more was a hand-painted sign hanging over a single door in the front.

"Sure don't look much like the places back home, does it?" grumbled Tex as he eyed the establishment suspiciously.

"You know what they say," said Slocum. "You can't judge a book by its cover."

McCoy ran a hand over his mustache, brushing away any sourdough crumbs that might have lodged there during his meal. "Well, I ain't read many books, but I have visited my share of gambling halls and bordellos. So I'll let you know what I think once I get inside and take a look around."

Slocum followed the Texan through the doorway, leaving the foggy boardwalk behind them. Their disappointment suddenly vanished. The barnlike structure was a veritable paradise for those who frequented saloons and brothels on a regular basis. A long bar stretched down one wall for fifty feet, and behind it stood three bartenders and shelf upon shelf of liquor bottles. In the center of the sawdust-covered floor were felt-topped tables offering every type of game of chance imaginable—poker, blackjack, faro, craps, and even roulette. Near the back of the cavernous room, where a number of private rooms had been built, sat a gathering of the most beautiful women that Slocum and McCoy had ever seen under one roof. They were dressed in bright silk, lace, and feathered plumes, and each was the picture of delicate femininity. From a quick glance, there looked to be a dozen or so lounging on velvet sofas or sitting at drinking tables with potential customers. Slocum wondered how many were absent from their posts, taking care of business in the honeycomb of rooms throughout the big warehouse.

"Not bad, if I do say so myself," said Tex McCoy with a big grin. "What do you want to do first, John? Drink, gamble, or screw?"

The walk across town had left Slocum's throat parched. "A shot of whiskey would go down good right about now."

Tex nodded. "My thoughts exactly." Together, the two drifters headed for the long bar at the far side of the Blue Orchid.

After buying a bottle of red-eye and two glasses to drink it out of, Slocum and McCoy walked around the crowded tables. Cards fluttered, dice were rolled, and the clacking of the steel ball in the roulette wheel could be heard. Tobacco smoke and the sour scent of liquor hung heavily in the air, along with the faint odor of French perfume that drifted teasingly from the soiled doves who awaited their turn at the rear of the room. Slocum and McCoy finally decided to start out with what they knew best—poker. They found a couple of empty chairs at a five-hand table and sat down, ready to test their prowess at the game.

They bought their chips from the dealer, then were dealt their first hands. It wasn't long before Slocum won the game, showing a royal flush when all the bets had been placed and all the cards played. The win was no real surprise to the Southerner. He wasn't a cardsharp, but he had learned a few tricks while frequenting gambling halls and riverboat casinos during the past several years.

The first game gradually grew into three or four. One by one, the players sensed that Lady Luck wasn't shining on them that night, and they folded, leaving the table for something more favorable. Tex threw in the towel after the fifth hand, his chips having dwindled down to less than a handful. With disgust, he tossed his cards down and sat back in his chair, anxious to see if Slocum would fare any better.

He did. The games grew more tense and the stakes much higher. Soon, Slocum's pot grew considerably richer, while those of the remaining players grew significantly poorer. Finally, the only one left to face the dark-haired Southerner was a crusty sailor with cold gray eyes and pockmarked cheeks. He held his cards close to the front of his navy pea coat, as if attempting to hide them from Slocum. But the drifter seemed to possess some uncanny ability for sensing which cards the seaman held. Bluff as he might, the sailor couldn't seem to get the upper hand on the tall Georgian.

When he finally lost his last dollar to Slocum, the seaman decided that he had been defeated by more than pure luck. "You're a damned cheat, that's what you are!" he growled, standing up so suddenly that he knocked his chair over.

Slocum simply sat there, sweeping his chips across the tabletop with both hands. "No sir," he replied calmly. "Just a helluva better poker player, that's all."

"I've played poker from Singapore to Cape Hope!" proclaimed the man bitterly. "And I beat every honest player I ever faced. I lost this time, so it must've been for a good reason." He reached out and fisted his big, calloused hand

around the neck of a whiskey bottle he had been emptying throughout the game. "I figure that reason to be clear
enough to everyone here at this table."

Slocum's green eyes glinted dangerously as he stared at
the angry seaman. "I'd advise you to put that bottle down
and walk out of here, before you come to regret it."

The sailor laughed. "Oh, is that so?" He brought the
bottle down sharply on the edge of the table, shattering
it in half. He waved the jagged edge menacingly. "We'll
see how bold you talk with half a face!"

Without another word of warning, the man attacked,
swinging the razor edge of the broken bottle toward the
drifter's head. But Slocum was ready for the move. He
stood up, lifting the poker table with him. The jagged spikes
of glass caught green felt instead of flesh, parting it cleanly
and scoring the wooden surface underneath.

As the man reared back for another swing, Slocum sidestepped the overturned table and came in close. He ducked
the deadly bottle as it made its second pass, then delivered
a powerful punch to the man's stomach. Bad breath and
spittle flew from the man's mouth as he doubled over.
The Southerner followed up with a well-placed blow to the
side of the sailor's jaw. With a grunt, the seaman released
the bottle from his grasp and fell on his back across the
sawdust floor.

"Slocum!" yelled Tex McCoy from the sidelines. "Behind
you!"

The Georgian whirled on his heels. Another sailor—
obviously a friend of the sore loser who had been playing
craps at a neighboring table—was approaching him swiftly,
holding a knife with a handle of scrimshawed ivory in his
hand. Slocum thought about drawing his gun, but knew
there was no time to slip the thong from the hammer.
Instead, he grabbed up a chair and blocked the man's

first swing with it. The edge of the blade scraped against the bottom of the chair, then was parried to the side with a sweep of the wooden legs.

Slocum was preparing to fend off any further attacks by the knife-wielding sailor, when he saw Tex step up behind the fellow. One crack across the skull from the barrel of McCoy's long-barreled Remington ended the fight right then and there. The seaman's eyes rolled back in his hand, and he dropped to the floor, landing across the sluggish form of his shipmate.

A moment later, a burly bouncer with a bald head, red beard, and a gold ring in one earlobe appeared from the direction of the bar. He lifted the two sailors roughly by their collars and, taking one in each hand, began to drag them toward the front door. "Did I not tell you two salts to behave yourselves in here?" bellowed the bouncer, whose accent seemed to be French-Canadian. "Well, it is outside with you now. And you'd best sober up and get back to your boat, before the wharf rats eat you alive!"

When the ruckus had died down, Slocum turned to his friend. "Much obliged for the help, Tex," he said. "Didn't see the fellow coming till he was nearly upon me."

"My pleasure, John," said the cowboy with a nod. He returned his revolver to its holster, then motioned toward the rear of the waterfront establishment. "I've grown tired of gambling for tonight. Why don't we partake of those pretty gals back yonder?"

"Sounds good to me," agreed Slocum. He had only spent an hour at the poker table, but his winning streak had been a profitable one. He cashed his chips in, then stuck a wad of greenbacks into the inside pocket of his coat.

They made their way past the gambling tables to the rear of the room. As they approached the women in the bright gowns and plumes, a buxom redhead who appeared to be in her late fifties met them. "Howdy, gents!" she said in welcome. "Nothing like a bare-knuckle brawl to whet a man's appetite for women, ain't that right?" she asked with a laugh.

Slocum ignored the madam's sales pitch. "How much?" he simply asked.

"Two dollars for two hours," she replied. "Five for all night."

"Sounds fair enough," said McCoy. He laid two silver dollars in the madam's hand. Slocum did the same.

"Very well, gentlemen," she said, depositing the coins in the cleft of her considerable cleavage. "Go on and take your pick. They're all clean and healthy, with no lice or clap to make your visit here a less than pleasant one. But I warn you, no rough stuff or you'll have to answer to Henri over there." She indicated the bald bouncer, who returned through the front door, rubbing his massive hands together.

"Don't worry, ma'am," said Tex. "We're a couple of perfect gentlemen."

The madam eyed Slocum from head to toe. "Well, one of you seems perfect enough at least."

The two moved past the madam and began to mingle among the lounging beauties. Tex found his partner almost at once—a tall, leggy blonde dressed in bright pink silk and black lace. Slocum was more choosy, though. He went from one to another, sizing them up, looking for the one that would be most worth his two dollars.

He found her a moment later. Standing in the beaded doorway that led into the huge whorehouse was a sleek, dark-haired woman in her early twenties. Her skin was brown like an Indian's, but her features were more delicate and her eyes were a peculiar almond shape, like those of an Oriental. She was dressed in a black bodice and garters, and evening gloves that stretched clear up to her elbows.

When the girl noticed his interest, she moved away from the entrance and approached him. She extended a gloved hand toward him. "My name is Selana," she said softly, her eyes like dark flames. He could see the desire there, burning just as brightly as that in his own eyes.

"Name's John," said Slocum, feeling himself stir as he took her hand in his. He nodded toward the curtain of glass beads. "Shall we?"

She tightened her grip on his fingers, drawing him away from the noise and smoke of the gambling hall. "Come with me."

Slocum surrendered himself to the mysterious woman named Selana. He glanced around, looking for some sign of McCoy, but the long, tall Texan had apparently already retired to the back with the skinny blonde. Slocum drew in a deep breath and savored Selana's perfume, which smelled like the sweetest of orchids. The scent was almost intoxicating as the dark-haired whore led him past the barrier of the beaded curtain, toward a dark corridor just beyond.

3

On his way down the rear hallway, Slocum really didn't know what to expect. Although the corridor was gloomy, there were lanterns hanging from the ceiling here and there, casting a dim glow on row after row of wooden doors. As they made their way to Selana's room, the tall Georgian could hear the harsh breathing and low moans of mounting pleasure echo from behind several of the partitions. The noises only increased the urgency of Slocum's own lust, making him realize just how long it had been since he had last been with a woman.

"Here we are," the dark-haired beauty said as she paused and opened a door near the far end of the hallway. Reaching out, she took Slocum's hand and drew him through the doorway into darkness. "Allow me a moment to light a lamp," she told him in a whispery voice that was smooth as silk. "You are my first visitor tonight."

As the woman lifted the chimney of an oil lamp and lit the wick, Slocum studied her loveliness in the soft glow, a loveliness that was strangely savage in nature. "That's hard to believe," he said with a smile. As he closed the door behind him, Slocum wrinkled his nose. "What's that godawful smell?"

"Whale oil," replied the whore, indicating the lamp. "It is much more common in San Francisco than coal oil."

Slocum nodded. "I reckon so." As he removed his hat

and coat, the drifter looked around the interior of the windowless room. He had not expected much—perhaps a lamp and a single cot, like many whorehouses boasted. But he was pleasantly surprised. The room had been provided with the finest furnishings money could buy. There was a huge brass-framed bed, an ornately carved wardrobe, a mirrored dresser with a porcelain pitcher and washbasin, and a dressing screen of delicate rice paper with an Oriental scene painted on its panels.

The dressing screen returned Slocum's thoughts to exactly what sort of woman Selana was. "Pardon me for asking," he said as he sat on the bed and pulled off his boots, "but exactly where do you hail from? You kind of look like an Indian, but then again you look a little Chinese, too."

The woman was not offended by his question. Instead, she seemed a little amused. "I am an Eskimo. I come from Alaska."

Slocum was surprised. He had heard a lot about the vast territory that bordered Canada in the northwest. He had heard stories of endless miles of untamed land and million-dollar gold strikes, from those who had been there and those who had the desire to go and seek their fortune. Slocum had even considered traveling to the icy regions of the territory himself someday, but not for the obvious reason. The Southerner didn't suffer from gold fever; he never had and probably never would. The lure of precious metal held no power over a drifter like Slocum. He was content with what little money he could live on from day to day. Rather, it was the call of the wild that interested him most. The thought of riding through a land that was, for the most part, completely unsettled appealed to his wandering spirit. Even the horror stories of freezing weather, starvation, and wild animals failed to put a damper on the desire to explore the unexplored that lingered in the far reaches of the back of his mind.

"They say it's a hostile land," he said, unbuttoning his shirt. "A land so cold that it can freeze a flame on the end of a candle."

"Oh, it can be cold," said Selana. Slowly, the Eskimo peeled away her gartered stockings, revealing long, brown legs. "But we manage to stay warm . . . one way or another."

"I can imagine," said Slocum with a smile. He shed his vest and shirt as the whore unfastened the hooks of her bodice. A moment later, Selana was totally revealed to him. Slocum sat there on the point of breathlessness. He had encountered many women during his time in the West, but the woman who stood before him that night certainly had to be one of the most beautiful. His eyes traveled past her lovely almond-shaped eyes to the lush fullness of her lips. They were not painted a garish red like many of the whores' lips at the Blue Orchid, but were naturally robust and rose-colored. He shifted his gaze down her swanlike neck, then lingered for a moment at the gentle swell of her bust. Selana's breasts weren't overly large, but they were large enough, and perfectly shaped, with dark brown nipples. Farther on his eyes drifted, past her flat stomach to the womanly curve of her hips. At the junction of her muscular thighs flared a triangle of silky black hair, neatly trimmed with a teasing trace of her opening peeking from the down. In the light of the lamp, Slocum could detect the gleam of wetness there. It pleased him to know that she was just as eager for their encounter as he was.

Selana turned and walked to a small table in the corner of the room, giving the Georgian an enticing view of her firm buttocks. She lifted a shot glass in one hand and a crystal decanter in another. "Would you care for a drink, John?"

"I had whiskey out in the gambling hall," said Slocum.

"That dreadful stuff?" she said with a frown. "That's for those nasty sailors. This is much better. Brandy imported straight from Europe."

Slocum was impressed. "Do you offer all your customers such fine liquor?"

Selana shook her head. "No, only those who would appreciate it."

"Then I'll take some."

The woman poured a couple of fingers of the amber liquor into the glass and brought it to him. "I hope you enjoy it."

"Aren't you joining me?" asked Slocum.

"I want to be fully alert for our time together," said Selana, her dark eyes sultry. "I mostly cater to stinking, fat-bellied drunks. Rarely do I get to pleasure a man as handsome as you."

Slocum stared into the woman's eyes as he swallowed the fancy liquor. He could tell that his interlude with the Eskimo woman would be one that he would remember for a very long time.

After finishing his drink, Slocum stood up. He unbuckled his gunbelt, slung it over the brass post of the bed, and then unbuttoned his trousers. Soon, his britches were pooled around his ankles, and he was as naked as the woman who stood before him. He kicked the clothing away, and a moment later, they clashed in an embrace that was both tender and urgent. Slocum groaned at the touch of Selana's smooth skin against him, while the woman moaned at the feeling of his hard muscles and roving hands against her own body.

Slocum wasted no time. He captured Selana's mouth with his own. Their lips meshed and their tongues entwined, exploring, tasting each other. Then his mouth traveled downward, along the lean column of her throat, until it reached the sloping mounds of her breasts. He grasped one in his hand and kneaded the circle of the areola until the nipple sprang forth. Then he took the hard bud between his lips and sucked.

Selana threw back her head and cried out. Her hands traveled down the muscular curve of Slocum's back, then moved around his narrow hips to his crotch. His manhood stood erect, but her fingers worked at it, stroking and pulling until it was even more than it had been. As Slocum shifted his mouth to her other nipple, her passion grew too powerful for her to control. She leapt upward, encircling his hips with her long legs, bearing him backward toward the bed.

As they fell to the feather mattress, Selana positioned herself deftly over the drifter's lower abdomen. Slocum surrendered and lay back, allowing her to take the reins. Other men might have felt differently, thinking that only a man had the right to serve as the aggressor in affairs of the flesh. But Slocum was a man who knew better. Some of the most pleasurable moments he had ever shared with women had come in such fits of insatiable abandon. He knew that Selana would prove to be equally satisfying as he felt her weight drop, inch by maddening inch, engulfing his rigid member in a pocket of hot wetness.

Slocum couldn't help but groan out loud. He reached up and kneaded the swinging pendulums of Selana's breasts as she rode him, her round hips churning, the inner walls of her sex gripping him like a tight fist. Slocum could endure the immobility of his position no longer. He grabbed the whore beneath the armpits and lifted her body upward. Then, with strong thrusts, he fed himself up to her.

The dark-haired whore screamed out as she was filled to her very depths. "I've never felt it . . . so *good*!" she rasped, her eyes clenched tightly shut.

Slocum had to admit that it had been a long time since he had been with a woman that drove him to passion as furiously as Selana did. He felt his balls tighten and his sap begin to rise. Knowing that he didn't have much time, he changed their position, shifting his weight and flipping the Eskimo woman onto her back. He drove into her powerfully with loud, wet slaps. Selana helped out the best that she could, lifting her hips up to meet him. Then, in a single explosion of ecstasy, both man and woman came together.

Wearily, Slocum rolled over onto his back and lay there, staring up at the ceiling. For some reason, his copulation with the dark-haired beauty had left him more than a little winded. Confused, he turned his eyes to the woman who reclined next to him. Selana simply lay there, staring back at him with an expression akin to regret.

Slocum sat up, then reached down, slipping his feet into the legs of his britches and tugging them up around his waist. As he stood and buttoned the fly, his head swam. Dizzily, he reached out and steadied himself with the brass footrail, attempting to even his balance before he fell down. Again, he looked at the whore, then shifted his gaze across the room to the crystal decanter.

At once, he knew what had happened. Selana had slipped him a drug of some kind.

"You bitch! What the hell have you done to me?" Slocum's mouth was open, but the words of accusation hadn't come from him. Instead, they'd come from the hallway beyond the door. He recognized the voice immediately. It belonged to his friend Tex McCoy.

Slocum staggered toward the brass post at the head of the bed, his fingers grasping sluggishly for the curved butt of his Colt Navy. But he was much too slow. Selana reached the gunbelt before him. She shucked the .36 revolver from its holster and, cocking the hammer, leveled the gun at Slocum. "I'm sorry, John," she said. "Really, I am."

At the sound of a commotion in the hallway, Slocum turned and stumbled toward the door. He wrenched it open and steadied himself in the door frame, looking down the hallway. Twelve feet away, Tex stood on trembling legs, the wrist of his blond whore in one hand and the long-barreled Remington .44 in the other. He was dressed only in his faded red longhandles and his ten-gallon hat.

McCoy's eyes met Slocum's at about the same time. "They've done something to me, John," he bellowed. "Drugged me with some poisoned hooch!"

Before Slocum could say anything in reply, a door opened at the end of the corridor. Two brawny men rushed down the hallway toward the unsteady cowboy, eager to shut him up. Tex whirled and shot blindly with his pistol. The big .44 roared, and one of the men went down on one knee, cursing and clasping a bloody hole in the bicep of his right arm. The other man, however, reached McCoy before he could fire again.

"Tex!" yelled Slocum, although his own voice seemed to echo from a mile away. "Look out!"

The Texan attempted to cock his Remington again, but his thumb wouldn't work the way he wanted it to. Abruptly, the man was upon the lanky cowboy. Something dark flashed in his hand, and Slocum saw that what he held was a leather blackjack. Once . . . twice . . . three times the lead-filled sap descended, flattening Tex's hat and crashing into the skull tucked inside. Slocum saw a dark stain widen on the felt of the hat, then his friend fell limply to the floor of the whorehouse hallway.

Slocum took a step into the corridor, ready to confront the attacker, despite his own weakened state. He wasn't given the chance. Suddenly, from the opposite end of the hall, someone reached out and, with a fist like a vise, grabbed him by the throat.

The Southerner found himself looking into the bearded face of the bouncer named Henri. "Got us some trouble here, do we now?" he said with a smirk. "I think not. No, it is you who are in for the trouble. Just you wait and see."

Slocum attempted to throw a punch at the man, but all the strength in his body seemed to have drained away. His fist met the bouncer's whiskered jaw with about as much force as a child stroking the head of a much-loved puppy. He felt his legs buckle underneath him, but before he could fall, Henri grabbed him beneath the arms. Seemingly with no effort at all, the burly Canadian toted Slocum down the hallway to where Tex lay in a heap.

"Open the trap!" said Henri, keeping his voice low. "Hurry!"

The thug with the blackjack nodded. Stepping back a couple of feet, he bent down and stuck his thick fingers through a crack in the floor. A second later, he had opened up a trapdoor in the center of the hallway. The portal looked as dark as death, and somewhere deep down within, Slocum thought he heard the distant lapping of water.

"Dump them in," ordered Henri. "Both of them."

Slocum wanted to fight and escape, but the chemical in the brandy he had drunk had sapped all his strength and willpower. Helplessly, he watched as Tex was tossed through the open trap. Next went his clothes and boots, brought from the room by the skinny blond whore.

"Now it is your turn, cowboy," said Henri. He dragged Slocum to the edge of the trapdoor. The Southerner stared down into the pit and heard McCoy as he finally reached the bottom. But, strangely enough, he failed to hear the splash of water. There was only a dull thud, as if McCoy had landed on some wooden platform that was hidden below.

Slocum turned his head toward the room he had just made love in. Selana stood in the doorway, still naked and holding his boots and clothing in her arms. He looked toward her face, to see if remorse remained there, but he couldn't tell. The drug was fogging his vision. Her features blurred, then began to dim to blackness.

The darkness that began to engulf Slocum was completed when he was thrown, head-first, through the trapdoor in the floor. Instead of meeting empty air, he found himself sliding down a wooden shoot of some sort. He attempted to stop his descent, but he could find no handhold. Faster and faster, he dropped down the passageway, the light from the corridor overhead moving farther away.

Slocum prepared himself for the impact of his arrival at the bottom, but he never felt it. Before he reached his destination, the darkness closed tightly around him and he passed out.

4

Slocum awoke to a blinding ache in his head and a queasiness in his stomach. The pain that pounded between his temples was due to the drug that the whore had slipped him. The sick sensation had a different origin, however. It took him a moment to realize that, for some strange reason, his body was in constant motion, gently swaying from side to side.

When he finally opened his eyes, he found that it wasn't actually he who moved, but rather the chamber that he was confined to. He peered through the gloom, adjusting his vision to the dim glow of a whale-oil lantern that hung from the ceiling overhead. The first thing he saw was the massive beams that stretched overhead, three times sturdier than the kind that would support the roof of a house. He then noticed that the wall he sat against was slightly curved, and the roughly hewn floor underneath him was damp to the touch.

As Slocum's eyes sharpened, he saw that he was not alone in the shadowy room. Others sat along the sloping wall as well, while a few lay on the floor, still in the clutches of their individual stupors. Slocum was aware of a constant roaring, as well as a monotonous creaking that echoed from somewhere overhead. He tried to identify the noises, but they were strangely alien to him.

"Where the hell am I?" he muttered. He shook his head,

attempting to drive the pain away, but he only aggravated it more.

"You're in the hold of a ship, my friend," came a voice from beside him.

At first, Slocum thought it was Tex McCoy who was speaking to him. But it couldn't be. The voice was much too cultured and possessed a decidedly Irish brogue. Careful not to swing his head too abruptly, Slocum glanced to his right and found a short, stocky fellow sitting next to him. He was dressed in fine Eastern duds, but the tailored clothing couldn't hide the brawn of his physique.

"A ship?" asked the Southerner, confused. "What are you talking about?"

"You've been duped, just like the rest of us," said the Irishman. "They held the lure of feminine flesh in front of us, and like the horny males we are, we took the bait— hook, line, and sinker."

Slocum's thoughts began to clear a little, and he examined his situation more closely. He was half-dressed, wearing only trousers and shirt, while his boots, hat, and coat lay next to him. He moved his legs in an attempt to sit up straighter and, for the first time, realized that his ankles were encased in shackles. Incredulously, he examined the heavy iron chain and found that it linked him to all the others in the hold.

It was at that moment that he realized the significance of the odd noises; the roaring was the sound of waves lapping against the hull of the ship, while the other noise was the wooden creak of a windswept mast overhead. A single word blazed through Slocum's thoughts, one that sent a thrill of desperation throughout the tall Georgian.

"Shanghaied!"

"Yes, sir," said the Irishman. "That certainly seems to be the nature of our predicament."

"But I thought those days were long past," said Slocum. "I haven't heard of men being taken against their will in years."

"Me either," said the man next to him. "But obviously the dastardly practice still takes place. After all, we are here, aren't we?"

Slocum grew silent. It had been a long time since he had heard of able-bodied men being shanghaied and put to work as slave laborers. He thought the practice had ended long before the War Between the States, but apparently he was mistaken.

As the throbbing in his head began to dull, he thought back to the last moments before he had passed out. He remembered the pleasure he had shared with Selana, as well as the blackjack-wielding bouncers and the ugly, bearded face of Henri. Then he remembered the lead-filled sap flattening a high-peeked hat, and the darkness of blood it had drawn. "Tex!" he said out loud.

"If you are referring to your rawboned friend, he is there next to you," said the Irishman. "Unfortunately, it seems that he got the worse of it, compared to the rest of us."

Slocum turned and stared at the lanky form next to him. Tex McCoy lay on the cold floor of the hold, curled up like a frightened child. His eyes were wide open, yet they seemed unfocused, as if they saw absolutely nothing. Slocum's attention was drawn by the crown of the Texan's head, and he cursed beneath his breath. The slope of McCoy's skull seemed to be oddly flat on one side, the skin over the spot darkly bruised and encrusted with dried blood.

"The sons of bitches!" growled Slocum. "What'd they do to you, Tex?"

He reached out, but when he laid his hand on Tex's arm, the man whimpered like a whipped dog and recoiled. The

eyes that had once stared across Texas plains and squinted against blowing dust storms darted from side to side,
frightened by the least little sound or movement. Slocum
turned away in disgust. It hurt him to see the rambunctious
cowboy in such a sorry state. He was afraid that whatever
damage had been done to Tex's head was permanent and
that the man he once knew was now lost forever.

"I'm sorry," said the Irishman as Slocum turned his angry
eyes back to him. "I suppose he proved to be more of a
fighter than the rest of us."

"Yeah, he did," agreed Slocum. He remembered Tex
standing in the rear hallway of the Blue Orchid, befuddled
by the drug he had been given, but able to wound one of the
bouncers with a shot from his Remington .44 nevertheless.
Slocum drove the image from his mind and studied the
Easterner. "What is your name?" he asked.

"Sean O'Brady," said the man, extending his hand. "I
hail from Pittsburgh, Pennsylvania."

Slocum took the man's hand and was surprised at how
strong the grip was. The pads of his hands were thick with
callouses, too. It was plain to see that O'Brady was not a
stranger to hard work. "I take it that your trade doesn't
match your fancy duds, does it?"

O'Brady laughed. "Mother O'Mary, no! To tell the truth,
I worked as an ironworker in the Pittsburgh mills since
the age of ten. And I'd probably still be slaving there if
I hadn't learned to read and educated myself. I quit my job
and took the first train out here, hoping to find something
better than those stinking iron pits. But where did I end
up instead? Confined in the dank hold of some rat-infested
ship, sailing for God knows where!" The Irishman regarded
his neighboring prisoner with interest. "And who might
you be?"

"Name's Slocum," said the Georgian, figuring it would

do no harm to reveal his true name. "John Slocum."

"Pleased to meet you," said O'Brady with a nod of his curly red head.

"Why don't you two pipe down over there!" came a deep voice from a support post that stood only a few yards away. "This ain't no time for socializing, you know. Whether you want to admit it or not, we're in a heap of trouble here. All of us."

Slocum studied the man who spoke. He was a big Negro, well over six feet tall and topping three hundred pounds in weight. Some of the black man's bulk was due to fat around his waist, but most of it was solid muscle that lay in dark slabs across his shoulders and arms. Apparently, whoever had imprisoned them in the hold had given his confinement a little more consideration. The Negro was bound hand and foot in shackles and chains, and his midsection was lashed to the support pole with heavy rope.

"Don't pay any attention to the spade over there," said O'Brady. "His name is Casey Elder, and he thinks he is above being in such a predicament."

"You better believe it, you dumb mick," grumbled the Negro. "I was a slave for ten years before Mr. Lincoln delivered me from that yoke. And I ain't about to be no white man's property again. I'd rather die first!"

"I'd watch what I say if I were you, Elder," said O'Brady. "If these seafaring mates who hog-tied us hear your bitching and complaining, they might cast you overboard. Then you'd be free, but you'd be food for the sharks as well."

"Quiet!" Slocum told both of them. "I think I hear someone coming."

Elder and O'Brady stopped their bickering. Every man in the hold listened as the sound of footsteps echoed from the opposite side of a door constructed of seasoned oak and heavy iron hinges. There was the rattle of a skeleton key in the lock, then the door swung inward. Two sailors in dark britches and striped shirts stepped inside, holding lanterns aloft. Next entered a tall, elderly man dressed in the dark blue uniform and cap of a ship's captain. He was a sour-looking gentleman with steel-gray eyes and muttonchop whiskers that grew into a mustache beneath his hawkish nose. As he walked through the hold, appraising the chained men with an air of superiority, he steadied himself with the help of a long blackthorn cane with the head of a snarling sea serpent carved into end of its crooked handle.

"Well, saints preserve us all!" whispered O'Brady softly. "If it isn't the man himself!"

"Who?" asked Slocum.

"Shanghai Kelly," said the Irishman, then he grew silent as the trio of seamen came toward them.

Slocum stared at the elderly man with the blackthorn cane. He had heard tales about the dastardly captain who shanghaied strong men with any means available and sold them as slaves to kings and sultans in foreign lands, sometimes to toil in gold and gem mines, other times to fight wars they had no business fighting in. But those old legends had been from another time, before the railroad and the telegraph had even come into being. Apparently, though, the tall tales had been truth rather than bunk, for the man was standing there, right in front of them.

Kelly walked past O'Brady and Slocum, nodding in approval. When he reached Tex McCoy's prone form, he prodded the cowboy with the tip of his cane and grunted sourly. "He will not do," muttered the captain. "Not at all."

"Want me to take him up on deck and pitch him over the bow?" asked one of the sailors.

"No," replied Shanghai Kelly. "He's damaged goods, but I should get a few pieces of silver for him nonetheless." He rested both of his wrinkled hands on the head of his cane and raked his steely eyes across the line of chained men. "Now, listen up and listen good, for this will be the only time we will talk during this voyage. You have a long journey ahead of you, several weeks in fact. You will be fed water and hardtack two times a day, and if you need to relieve yourselves, buckets have been provided for that purpose. Some of you will suffer seasickness and, more than likely, will not survive to see our destination. The rest will be unloaded at the port of St. Michael in order to serve your new master."

At first, Slocum didn't recognize the name of the seaport. Then it came to him. St. Michael was located on the coast of the territory called Alaska. He recalled his encounter with the Eskimo whore named Selana and wondered if her part in his abduction had a direct link to where he was eventually bound for.

"And who is this scoundrel we will be sold to?" asked Sean O'Brady boldly.

"The gentleman who commissioned your capture is an extremely wealthy man by the name of King," said Kelly. "And if you know what's good for you, I would suggest that you keep that glib tongue to yourself."

"He's right, Irishman," came a familiar voice from the open doorway. "Mr. King is not a man to be meddled with. I have killed men for him simply because they looked at him in the wrong manner. And I will do so again, if he tells me to."

Slocum looked at the big man standing in the doorway and instantly bristled. It was Henri, the bearded bouncer from the Blue Orchid, the one who had personally dumped him through the trapdoor in the bordello floor. Slocum's rage burned, and his right hand ached for the feel of the Colt Navy in its palm. His anger was stoked even hotter when he spotted his revolver in the bouncer's possession. It was stuck in the waistband of Henri's trousers, along with McCoy's long-barreled Remington.

"Listen to him, gentlemen," said Shanghai Kelly. "Mr. Gastineau is telling the truth. Death awaits those who disobey the man or his foremen. Heed my warning and you just might live to reach a ripe old age."

And with that, the elderly captain turned and left. Henri Gastineau and the two sailors followed, closing the heavy door behind them. The men chained along the wall of the ship's hold were deathly silent as the footsteps faded, heading upward toward the deck.

"I wonder what this King feller has in mind for us," Slocum said, finally breaking the silence.

"Well, if Alaska is involved, I certainly have a good idea," said O'Brady, his wry features creased with a grim seriousness.

Slocum thought about it for a moment, then nodded. "Gold," he said. He looked around at the men who filled the hold, close to thirty or forty in number. "And from the looks of it, I'd say this King feller has a mighty big strike to be mined."

5

Shanghai Kelly was right. Slocum and his fellow prisoners were in for one rough and treacherous journey.

After the ship had left port at San Francisco and began its voyage along the northwestern coast, time seemed almost to stand still in the dark belly of the hold. There was no outside light to distinguish day from night, so no one had any idea what time it might be at any given hour. Any timepieces the men might have carried before their abduction had been taken away from them, along with all their other valuables.

Days stretched into weeks. The monotony of the long trip was punctuated with moments of fear and despair. Mostly the men divided their time between sleeping and talking. As promised by the ship's captain, meals were served, but they consisted of no more sustenance than a dipper of brackish water and a handful of lumpy rice or dry hardtack. Their diet was not the most nourishing, so many of the prisoners suffered from bouts of dysentery and severe nausea. The constant motion of the ocean beneath them failed to help matters any. Before the ship was three days out of port, the hold stank like the pit of a sewer, its air rank with the stench of vomit and defecation.

Also, as Kelly had predicted, some of the men in the hold succumbed to the sickness that gripped them. Given that it was winter on the high seas, the depths of the ship were as cold as an icebox. A few died of the fever of influenza, while others suffocated to death, their lungs unable to function due to pneumonia. Most of those who passed away were carried to the deck above by the ship's sailors and unceremoniously dumped overboard. Others were forgotten or overlooked. Before long, they began to decompose, drawing the rats from out of the rafters overhead. The rodents feasted on those who had died, and sometimes, when they grew hungry and bold enough, they attacked the living while they slept. Several times, Slocum awoke to find two or three rats nibbling at the arms and legs of Tex McCoy. The injured cowboy simply whimpered and cried like a helpless infant, afraid to defend himself against the scavengers. Slocum reacted with outrage and replusion, however. He would scream and rave, batting the brave rodents away with his fists, hoping to keep them at bay until their fear of him faded and they grew bold once again.

Once, nearly a week and a half into the voyage, the ship was caught up in the middle of a terrible storm. A gale of incredible force buffeted the vessel, causing it to bob along the violent waves like a cork in a rain-swollen creek. Lightning and thunder crashed overhead, echoing deafeningly, even in the lower reaches of the ship, and torrential rains and hail the size of grapeshot pelted the upper deck. Kelly's ship, however, survived the storm intact, and they continued onward, hoping to reach their destination by the end of December.

Toward the end of their voyage, Kelly's ship finally left the vast waters of the Pacific Ocean, passing the broken chain of the Aleutian Islands and entering the Bering Sea. The temperature dropped considerably, and the prisoners in the hold were given heavy woolen coats, as well as hot

coffee and warm food. The considerations were not due
to any compassion on the part of the evil captain, but
merely designed to protect his dwindling investment. By
Slocum's count, there had been forty-eight men confined to
the hold when the ship left San Francisco, and now, nearly
twenty days later, that number had dropped to a total of
thirty-six.

On the day of their arrival at St. Michael, a dozen of
Kelly's crew entered the hold of the ship, armed with rifles
and wooden bludgeons. Before their appearance, Slocum
and O'Brady had considered the possibility of rushing the
men who came for them and attempting an escape. But as
one man unshackled each prisoner while the other eleven
stood alertly on guard, they knew that it would be foolish to
do so. Kelly's crew looked to be men who had participated
in the captain's shanghai operation for a long time, seamen
who would be loyal to their leader, even if it led to their
deaths. Besides, even if they could have overpowered the
crew in the hold, there was no guarantee that they would
be as successful when they reached the deck above. There
could be fifty more waiting there, ready to shoot or club
them to death, then toss them overboard.

One by one, the prisoners were released from the shackles around their ankles. Then, just as swiftly, thick bracelets
of iron were clamped upon their wrists, linked together by
a short length of heavy chain. When they reached the prone
form of Tex McCoy, one of the seamen yelled for him to
sit up. After McCoy failed to respond, the sailor prodded
the cowboy in the small of the back with the muzzle of his
rifle. "You'd best do as they say," Slocum told him, then,
with the help of Sean O'Brady, he helped the wounded man
to his feet. Tex stood there, his eyes dull, as the shackles
were snapped around his wrists. It seemed as if he had no
comprehension of what was happening to him.

After all the other men were fitted with handcuffs, Kelly's crewmen gathered around Casey Elder. The big Negro cussed at them, then spat in the face of the sailor who held the key. One crewman stepped up and delivered a single blow to Elder's head, hitting him squarely between the eyes. The blow rattled the black man enough to calm him down, but did not knock him cold. Slocum couldn't help but think that such a blow would have killed an ordinary man.

Quickly, they went to work. They untied him and unfurled the length of heavy rope, but kept the wrist and ankle irons in place. Then the crew took their positions around the group of thirty-six men and carefully escorted them through the doorway of the ship's hold. As they were led along a narrow staircase to the upper deck, Slocum again gauged the chance for escape. There was none. Everywhere he looked there was a rifle with the hammer cocked and a crewman's finger poised over the trigger.

When they finally exited the hatch and stood upon the deck, they found the boards to be slick and icy. Several prisoners slipped and fell, but were quickly hustled to their feet again, prodded by the threat of a bullet to the brainpan. Slocum almost lost his footing, but regained his balance as they were herded to the railing of the bow. As he grabbed hold of the frosty rail to steady himself, the Southerner couldn't believe how bitterly cold it was outside the ship. Slocum had been in many a Western blizzard, but none could match the frigid temperatures that hovered around him at that moment. It was so cold that his breath was nearly taken away.

"Here!" demanded the familiar voice of Henri Gastineau. "Put these on, before you freeze to death."

Slocum turned and glared at the French-Canadian, who was dressed in a coat of heavy fur and a beaver cap with ear-flaps. Then he shifted his attention to a pile of secondhand clothing that was heaped on the icy deck. One by one, the men Slocum had spent several weeks in imprisonment with went to the pile and rummaged through the articles of warm clothing. When it was Slocum's turn, he quickly found a pair of cowhide gloves and a thick woolen scarf. He wasted no time in putting them to good use. Once they were on, they cut the discomfort of the sub-zero weather somewhat, if not completely.

Soon, every man on the deck was outfitted with warm clothing. Then they were lined up along the far railing and told to wait. A moment later, the door to the captain's cabin opened. Shanghai Kelly stepped outside, followed by a woman dressed in a frilly blue dress and veiled bonnet. Although the dark net of the veil obscured the female's features, Slocum knew by the jet black of her hair and the delicate curves of her form that it was none other than the whore named Selana. Escorted across the icy deck by the elderly captain, the Eskimo woman failed to give the chained men a second glance. Her dark eyes peered straight ahead, as if they didn't even exist. Slocum couldn't tell whether her actions were due to remorse on her part, or if she just didn't give a damn.

When Kelly and Selana had made their way down the gangplank to the dock below, Slocum turned his attention over the rail of the ship's bow. He stared across the icy waters of Norton Sound. Land surrounded the bay on three sides, then gave way to the emptiness of open sea. Somewhere in that general direction lay hundreds of miles of ocean and the port of San Francisco. In the drifter's eyes, they could have just as well docked in some foreign port in Australia or China. He was still a world away from the land he had roamed for the past two decades.

Slocum then turned his gaze along the shoreline. The settlement of St. Michael was small, but bustling with the activity of a boomtown. New buildings of unpainted lumber outnumbered older structures by two to one. Their construction, however, seemed to have been slowed by the coming of the Alaskan winter. Snow lay heavily on pitched roofs, and icicles that were several feet in length hung from the eaves of porches. Even though the intense cold numbed Slocum's nose, he could still sense the smells that were common of a seaport: the salty spray of the sea, the stench of fish, and the sooty tang of woodsmoke drifting from chimneys and stovepipes.

"All right, listen up!" roared the voice of Gastineau, drawing Slocum's attention back to the man with the thick red beard. "You'll be going to meet your master now. We'll be walking through town, and there is sure to be folks gawking at you. Heed my words and you'll make it to the far end of the city alive. Do not say a single word. If you try to yell out for help, you will be shot down immediately. For all the citizens of St. Michael know, you are merely inmates of a California prison sent here to work in the gold mines. If you try to convince them otherwise, you will die because of it. Do you understand?"

The gathering of shackled men grumbled in agreement. Slocum again eyed the crewmen with their lever-action rifles and knew that Gastineau was not lying. If anyone stepped out of line, he would pay for his mistake with his life.

"Very well!" said the burly Canadian. "Then let's go!"

In single file, the men who had been drugged by the whores of the Blue Orchid and shipped like cattle in the belly of Shanghai Kelly's renegade schooner began to make their way down the gangplank to the snowy dock below.

6

The walk they took through the center of St. Michael seemed to be the longest one that John Slocum ever endured.

The bitter cold of the Alaska wind and the iciness of the snow through the soles of his boots were only a small part of it. What angered him the most was the way the citizens of the seaport town studied him and the others with a mixture of repulsion and fear. He wanted nothing more than to yell out at them, tell them that he and the other men were not lawless scoundrels, but ordinary men who had been wrongly abducted and were now on their way to a life of slavery. But, despite his desire to do so, Slocum swallowed his words and continued his march along the snowy streets in silence. He knew that if he spoke up, Kelly's men would react, swiftly and with deadly precision.

Ever aware of the rifle muzzles directed at them, the group of shackled men made their way past the rows of storefronts, until they crossed a bridge over a frozen stream. On the other side stretched a gathering of homes, both affluent and poverty-stricken. First were the ramshackle sheds of weathered lumber and tin. They were the winter dwellings of tenderfoots who had come to Alaska in search of their fortune but found that their dreams were not nearly as easily acquired as they had first expected. Some sported only a single door and window, along with the sooty stovepipe of an iron potbelly that warmed the single room inside. Old newspapers undoubtedly lined the inner walls, acting as insulation against the cold that threatened to creep through the cracks between the boards.

Farther on stood the more substantial structures of the "sourdoughs," those who had lasted a winter or two in the hostile territory and had even benefited from the gold rush, perhaps sifting through a ton or two of earth to find a few random nuggets. Their houses were sturdier and possessed more than one room. The majority belonged to the businessmen and professionals who had journeyed to St. Michael in order to cash in on the needs of others. They were the ones who owned the biggest stake in the coastal town: the shopkeepers, doctors, and attorneys who provided their services in exchange for a bag full of gold dust or a percentage of some poor debtor's claim.

The homes closest to the boundries of St. Michael were those of men who had fought for their share of Alaska's bounty, or had even gone as far as lying and cheating for it. Swindlers lived in those fine homes of immaculate brick and marble, as well as cold-blooded murderers. While those who had suffered at the mercy of the greedy huddled in their cold shacks, barely able to feed themselves, the rich sat in their warm parlors, sipping imported liquor and totaling the contents of their money boxes.

It was one such house where Slocum and his fellow prisoners were herded. The structure was several stories high and possessed tall Greek columns of marble that had been shipped to Alaska by way of steamer ships. The place was as virginally white as the snow that wreathed it on all sides, yet it held a distinctive air of depravity and dishonesty, as if Satan himself had laid the mortar for its foundation.

As Slocum and the others approached the open gate of the mansion, the tall Southerner saw a fine black coach drawn by a brace of equally dark stallions come to a halt in front of the structure. Slocum watched as Shanghai Kelly and Selana left the shelter of the carriage and quickly rushed inside, eager to leave the frigid temperatures of that December afternoon behind them. Obviously, the fancy coach had picked up the captain and the whore before Slocum and the others had left the ship.

Slocum half expected to be marched through the front entrance as well, but he was mistaken. Instead, the prisoners were directed around the northern end of the manor house. Soon, they arrived at a cavernous structure that resembled a large stock barn. As they filed through the double doors, Slocum found that the place was an oversized stable. Several carriages stood in the center of the structure, surrounded on two sides by stalls of fine horses. The animals were all thoroughbreds, that was plain to see. Slocum had attended enough races in Kentucky to know a fine specimen of horseflesh when he saw one.

Henri Gastineau ordered the men to stop in the center of the structure. They waited there in the drafty building for several minutes, before two men entered the stable through a side door.

Both men were entirely different, both in physical stature and social bearing. One was a tall, broad-shouldered man with almond-shaped eyes and dark skin. Slocum pegged him as an Eskimo right off, for he possessed the same characteristics as Selana. He was obviously not a man to be trifled with. A Bowie knife with a scrimshawed handle protruded from the sash of his bearskin coat, and he carried a large-bore Sharps rifle in one massive hand. He also carried something lashed across his back by a beaded strap—a long bow and a quiver of arrows. They were slightly different than those of the Sioux or Comanche, but Slocum was certain that they were just as deadly in the capable hands of the towering Alaskan.

The other man was obviously the one responsible for their abduction and imprisonment. He, too, was a big man, but his bulk was due more to girth than height and muscle. He was obese, weighing well over three hundred and fifty pounds. The fine European suit that he wore looked as if it had been sewn by a circus tent-maker, instead of a tailor. He wore a gray derby hat and held a gold-headed cane in one pudgy hand, more for show than for actual use. His face was broad and ruddy, and sported a silver mustache and goatee beard. His were the features of an aristocrat, a man of breeding and lavish taste. And, much to his disgust, Slocum knew that he was also a man accustomed to buying whatever he fancied . . . even if that included men to labor for his greedy benefit.

The fat man nodded to Gastineau, then turned toward the men gathered before him. His eyes held a mixture of boredom and disdain as he strolled along the line, judging each man's size and strength. When he had finished his inspection, he turned and walked to a flatbed wagon that stood in the center of the stable. With the help of Gastineau and the Eskimo, the man climbed up on the wooden bed and stood there, looking like a king regarding his lowly subjects.

"My name is Arthur King," he said with a distinctively British accent. "I am the richest man in St. Michael . . . perhaps even the richest man in the territory of Alaska. I obtained that title through the pursuit of wealth, no matter what methods I might implement to attain it. In the past, it has meant stepping outside the normal boundaries of the law and recruiting laborers for my various enterprises, be it gold, furs, or whaling."

Slocum half expected Sean O'Brady to voice his opinion of the pompous Englishman, but he didn't. The Georgian glanced over to see the scrappy Irishman standing as still as stone, his eyes blazing with rage, but his face void of emotion. Apparently he knew when it was best to keep his mouth shut, and now was such a time.

"So, unfortunately for you," continued King, "my supply of able-bodied workers has recently reached a critical point. This was due to several reasons. Some died in unforeseen mishaps during the course of their duties, while others succumbed to disease or exposure to the harsh elements of this hostile land. Others died due to their own stupidity or pride. They bled to death at the lash of the whip or the shot of a rifle. That is something that all of you must keep foremost in your minds. Disobedience begets punishment. Give me a hard day's work and you will survive. Show laziness and disrespect toward those in charge of you, and you will suffer gravely. Mr. Gastineau and Kolabuk here will be your masters where you are going. To show disrespect toward them is to show it toward me. And that could give you fifty lashes with a bullwhip or a bullet between the eyes."

Slocum searched the Englishman's face, but knew that there was no bluff to the overweight dandy. He meant what he said. If anyone failed to meet his potential in whatever hell they were to be confined to, he would pay dearly for the trouble he caused.

"As for your eventual destination, my current lack of manpower is at my largest gold mine several hundred miles northeast of here. It is called the Glory Hole, which, for myself, it most certainly is. For you, it will seem like purgatory. Those of you who survive the journey and live to make it there will be expected to work as you have never worked before, perhaps fifteen or sixteen hours a day. And if you fail to mine your individual quotas of gold, you will be denied a blanket for the night and the following day's ration of food. And that can prove to be a fatal mistake to make, especially in the icy depths of the Glory Hole."

Slocum shifted his eyes to the man at the far end of the line—the big Negro that Kelly's crew had kept in ropes and chains. Like O'Brady, Elder knew when to hold his tongue. He looked as if he were on the verge of cussing the fat man for all he was worth, but fortunately he refrained from acting on his emotions.

"Very well," said Arthur King with a nod of his head. "That is all that I really have to say to you. Work as you are expected to, and you could very well live for several more years. Disappoint me, and your stay at the Glory Hole will be a short one, due to the circumstances of your death." And, with that, King left the wagon bed and, accompanied by the Eskimo named Kolabuk, left the way that he had entered.

Slocum couldn't believe the gall of the man. Just thinking of the offhand way he had detailed their life imprisonment and the fate they would suffer if they showed disobedience caused the Southerner to bristle in anger. Again, his right hand yearned for the smooth curve of the Navy pistol's butt and the weight of its loaded frame in his grasp.

"All right, you've all heard the man lay down his law!" said Gastineau. "Now find yourself a spot and settle down. You'll need your rest tonight, for we have a treacherous journey ahead of us tomorrow at dawn."

Reluctantly, the thirty-six men who had survived the voyage from San Francisco did as they were told. They crouched in the drafty confines of the stable, their thoughts grave and full of despair. Escape was, of course, contemplated, but not acted upon. To do so would surely bring instant death from the muzzles of a dozen well-aimed rifles.

Arthur King entered his mansion through a rear hallway. He rubbed the bite of the cold from his hands and made his way down a corridor decorated with ancient tapestries and tarnished suits of armor. Kolabuk followed him like a faithful but savage dog, ready to wreak havoc at his master's command.

A moment later, King walked into a lavish study paneled in oak and decorated with the heads of a dozen trophy animals, including Kodiak bear, African lion, and Indian tiger. Shanghai Kelly stood near a bay window, staring out at the frozen landscape beyond the town limits. The woman named Selana sat primly on a velvet divan, looking more than a little nervous.

When King entered the room, both of its occupants turned toward him. The sea captain regarded his client shrewdly, looking forward to being paid for the cargo he had delivered. Selana stood up, wringing her dainty hands. She attempted a sincere smile when King made his appearance, but failed miserably at the effort.

"It is good to see you again, Captain," said King, crossing the room and vigorously shaking the hand of the elderly seaman.

"My sentiments exactly," replied Kelly. "Have you had a chance to look over the merchandise?"

"Yes, I have, and I commend you on the quality, even though the quantity was much less than I anticipated."

Kelly shrugged. "The voyage was a long and trying one, Mr. King. Losses should be expected."

Arthur King nodded. He turned and regarded the lovely dark-haired woman in the blue dress. "Selana, my dear," he said as he walked toward her. "It is so very good to have you back home again."

"It is good to be back," she said, trying to make her words sound like anything other than the lie that they were. She shuddered slightly when the fat man embraced her and kissed her on the lips. Selana felt sick to her stomach. Given a choice, she would have rather been forced to swallow raw whale blubber than be touched by the man named Arthur King.

"I suppose you are anxious to be paid," said King to the sea captain. He left Selana and, rounding a huge desk, sat down in a leather-upholstered chair.

Shanghai Kelly smiled grimly. "I certainly didn't go through the trouble of rounding up those men for the sheer pleasure of it," he replied.

King laughed heartily. "No, I suppose not." He unlocked a side drawer, then withdrew a heavy metal box. He produced another key and, soon, the box was open. "What sort of currency do you prefer, Captain?"

"Gold," Kelly said flatly. "Minted or otherwise, it doesn't matter to me. Just so I'm well paid."

"Oh, you certainly shall be," agreed King. Meticulously, he set three stacks of golden eagles on the edge of the desk.

The captain's steely eyes gleamed with naked greed. But as he reached out to claim his reward, Arthur King quickly snatched two of the twenty-dollar pieces from the top of one stack. "Why did you do that?" asked Kelly, annoyed.

"I'm deducting it for damaged goods," said King. "The cowboy with the dent in his head."

The elderly captain opened his mouth, as if on the verge of expressing his displeasure. But he didn't. He sent a glance toward Kolabuk, who stood at the door, his right hand resting on the etched hilt of his Bowie, then graciously accepted the loss. With a single sweep of his wrinkled hand, the stacks of gold slid into the side pocket of his coat with a loud jingle.

"It was a pleasure doing business with you, Captain," said King with a smug grin. "I'll contact you if I require your services again. By the way, I do hope that you'll lend me the use of your crewmen for tonight. I wouldn't want my investment to slip through my fingers before I could put it to proper use."

"You can have them until dawn tomorrow," said Kelly. "But, after that, you must provide guards of your own."

"I assure you, I already have that taken care of."

Shanghai Kelly nodded to the obese Englishman, then slipped his cap over his gray head and left the room, several thousand dollars richer than he had been only a few minutes before.

Arthur King locked his money box and returned it to the desk drawer. After that task had been performed, he sat in his leather chair and stared at the woman on the couch for a long moment. Selana averted her lovely eyes, well aware of what he had in mind.

"Kolabuk," said King, failing to take his eyes off the woman for even a second, "I want you to go out to the stable and check out the sleds for tomorrow's journey to the Glory Hole. And feed the dogs an extra helping of venison tonight. I want them to be ready to run first thing in the morning."

"Yes sir, Mr. King," said the Eskimo in a rumbling voice. Before he left the room, he regarded the dark-haired woman with an expression akin to amusement. In turn, Selana glared back at him scornfully, as if she hated him even more than the Englishman who sat behind the desk.

Once Kolabuk had closed the door securely behind him, King stood up and walked around the desk, making his way toward the velvet divan. "I've missed you, Selana," he said. "Tell me, truthfully, did you miss me as well?"

The woman forced a smile. "Why, of course I did."

King met Selana's smile with one of his own, then brutally backhanded her, rocking her head and bringing a red welp to the left side of her beautiful face. "Truthfully, I said," he reminded with a cruel chuckle.

The smile faded from Selana's face, and raw contempt blazed in her dark eyes. "No," she said. "Actually, I despised the very thought of coming back to you."

King laughed uproariously. "Yes, I suppose that you did." He moved in closer, his bulk throwing a huge shadow across the cowering woman. "Tell me something, my dear. Did you enjoy the mission I sent you on? Did you enjoy rutting like a doe in heat with those drunken bums and saddle tramps?"

Selana lowered her eyes to the delicate pattern of the Oriental rug, ashamed to look him in the face. "No. I hated every moment of it."

The Englishman looked astonished. "Really now? And I suppose it was because of me. You felt guilty for being unfaithful to your husband, is that it?"

Selana said nothing. The fact that she was legally bound to the pompous businessman was hurtful even to think about, particularly the way in which the union had come to be.

"If that's the case, then you can make up for it right now," he said slyly. Before she knew it, he was over her, one hand pressed roughly against the swell of her bosom, the other pulling down the leggings of her frilly petticoat.

The woman wanted to scream and cry out in protest, but she didn't. She knew that it was no use, for no one at the King household would come to her rescue. Kolabuk was of her own kind, but after all, he had been the one responsible for her legal enslavement to the Englishman. And King's servants were totally loyal to him. They would ignore her cries and go on about their daily duties.

So she lay there on the divan and closed her eyes as she heard the rustle of King's britches being unbuttoned. Then his massive body was on top of her, crushing her into the cushions of the expensive sofa. She felt him search for her, poking and prodding until he found his way in. His thrusts were brutal and completely self-serving, and his breath stank of imported bourbon and Cuban cigars. Fortunately for Selana, the act of lust didn't last very long. Only a minute or so had passed before he spent his load and withdrew from her. A moment later, his weighty form was off of her and she could breath freely again.

Arthur King tucked himself back into his trousers and buttoned the fly. "Always remember, Selana, I own you body and soul, just as I own this fine mansion and that stable of thoroughbred horses out back. If you ever think of trying to run away, I'll send Kolabuk after you. And I'm sure you know what he is likely to do to you under such circumstances."

Selana swallowed nervously. She knew what the Eskimo punishment for infidelity was. Kolabuk would find her wherever she hid and cut the nose off her face. And, knowing King, the fat bastard would probably display it in his den, alongside all his other trophies.

"I assume you've gotten the message," said King, turning back to his desk. "Now, make yourself decent and go to your room. I have other business to attend to this afternoon."

Feeling like the whore she had been forced to become, Selana pulled up her undergarments and straightened the hem of her dress. As she crossed the room and opened the door, she glanced back at Arthur King. The Englishman had spent his lust and was now back to business as usual. He donned a pair of wire-rimmed spectacles and shuffled through a pile of deeds and legal documents that stood waiting in the center of his desk.

Selana recalled the life she had lived before she had been sold to King: her parents, their home on the bend of the Tanana River, and the man she had truly been in love with. Those things seemed to be a lifetime of pain and humiliation away at that moment. In despair, she slammed the study door behind her and, in tears, fled up the winding staircase to her bedroom.

7

Slocum was jolted awake by the prodding of a rifle barrel against his rib cage. "Wake up!" demanded the big Eskimo named Kolabuk. "Time to go!"

The drifter sat up and shook the fog of sleep from his mind. It was still dark. Lanterns glowed along the support beams of the huge stable, and no light shone around the shuttered windows or double doors. Slocum glanced around and saw that his fellow prisoners were also being rudely roused, with the hard muzzles of Winchesters or the toes of heavy leather boots.

By the time Slocum turned his attention back to the man who had awakened him, the hulking Eskimo had moved on to the next in line. For a split second, Slocum saw a chance at catching the man off guard. As Kolabuk leaned over to wake up Sean O'Brady, Slocum could have easily jumped up and, wrapping the chain of his shackles around the man's thick neck, choked the Eskimo until he lost hold of his Sharps rifle. But an instant later the chance had passed. Even if he had been in the position to jump the big man, Slocum knew that it would have turned out to be a foolish move on his part. Before he could even cock the hammer of the 50-caliber rifle, he would have been fired upon several times over. More than likely he would have ended up bleeding to death on the earthen floor of the stable, torn open by half a dozen bullets.

Slocum drove the disturbing image from his mind and, along with the others, rose to his feet. Several large wood stoves stood at key places in the stock barn, put there solely to keep Arthur King's collection of prized horses from freezing to death. But even with the stoves stoked to capacity, the stable was still cold. A frosty cloud of vapor exited from Slocum's lungs with each breath he took.

They were fed a quick breakfast of oatmeal and stale bread, then told to bundle up. After they had done so, the double doors were opened and Kelly's crewmen herded them outside into the frigid cold of early morning.

In front of the horse stable stood five long sleds of light wood. Each was loaded with crates of supplies, bound down securely with rope and tarpaulin. To the front of the sleds were harnessed teams of dogs six positioned in single file. Slocum had never seen dogs such as these before. They looked like a cross between a shepherd dog and a wolf. They were outfitted for the harsh terrain they would soon be crossing. Their coats were thick and warm, and the pads of their feet had been covered with man-made moccasins of caribou hide, soft and pliable, yet tough and insulated against the coldness of snow and ice.

A group of eight rugged men who stood nearby. Obviously, they would be the ones who replaced the guards that Shanghai Kelly had provided since their departure from the ship. The tall Georgian studied the eight. Three were white men, while the other five were Eskimo. All were hardcases—men who would not hesitate to unsheath a knife or bust a cap on anyone who gave them trouble— and all were armed to the teeth with shotguns, rifles, and large-caliber hoglegs.

Henri Gastineau appeared from around the corner of the stable. He walked to the group of guards and talked to them for a moment, his voice too low to overhear. Then he looked up at the sky, which was gradually changing from starry black velvet to a lightening gray, and double-checked the time with the aid of a gold pocket watch that dangled from the folds of his heavy fur coat.

"The son of a bitch has my papa's timepiece," grumbled Sean O'Brady beneath his breath. "The one he gave me while he lay upon his deathbed!"

Slocum nodded grimly. He knew what it was like to see a man carrying around property that wasn't rightfully his own. The Colt Navy revolver still protruded from the sash of Gastineau's coat. Slocum had a strong attachment to the 36-caliber revolver. He had carried it since the bloody days of the War Between the States. And he had put it to use more times than he could honestly remember, mostly against cutthroat scoundrals like Henri Gastineau and Kolabuk. He recalled the myth that the dime novels had perpetrated about a gunfighter carving notches on his gun to keep count of the men he had gunned down. If John Slocum had done such a thing, the Colt Navy would have been little more than a pile of steel dust and walnut shavings.

With a swagger, the French-Canadian left his confederates and walked toward the men destined for King's Glory Hole. Strapped to his feet were snowshoes, constructed of bowed birch and taut strips of tanned hide. "All right, you men, listen up! Three hundred and fifty miles of frozen wilderness lies between here and the place where you will spend the rest of your miserable lives. And you will be traveling every step of the way by foot. There's a stack of snowshoes there next to the woodpile. Strap a pair on, and if you've never walked with the aid of the contraptions before, you had best learn fast. We will be on our way in fifteen minutes."

One by one, the prisoners retrieved pairs of the awkward-looking shoes from the pile and lashed them to their boots with buckles and straps. Many of the men fell flat on their faces after their first steps, but Slocum was not among them. He had worn snowshoes before, in the upper reaches of the snowy Rockies. In deep drifts, the oblong frames prevented a man from sinking to his waist in snow. Obviously, there were such hazards awaiting them on the long journey northeast to King's gold mine.

After all the prisoners had been outfitted with snowshoes, Gastineau's troop of guards cautiously went to work. They split the thirty-six captives into groups of seven. Then, connecting a single length of rope to the shackles around their wrists, each group was tied to the frame of a dog sled. "I suggest that you keep up your pace, even if you grow weary," advised Gastineau. "These dogs run at an even clip. If you fail to match them, step by step, you will likely trip and fall. And, I warn you now, we will not stop for stragglers."

After all the preparations for the journey had been made, it was time to go. Henri Gastineau took the helm of one sled, while Kolabuk and three other Eskimos commandeered the others. Whips snapped crisply in the winter air, and the lead dogs leapt into motion at the call of "Mush!"

Soon, all five sleds and their tethers of shackled men began the long and treacherous journey across the frozen earth. The dogs began to pick up speed, and it wasn't long before the captives had to practically run to keep up. Some stumbled, but fortunately none fell. They all knew that to falter would mean being dragged alive across the rugged landscape of deep snow and hard ice.

A hundred yards from the horse stable, Gastineau yelled, "Gee!" On command, the lead dog of his team shifted direction, heading slightly to the right and to the east. Kolabuk and the others followed suit. In single file, the sleds and their human cargo left the civilized cradle of St.

Michael and set out for the harshest and most unforgiving wilderness known to man.

Slocum, who was chained to the rope that trailed from Gastineau's sled, looked over his shoulder only once before their departure. He saw the immaculate manor house of Arthur King standing picturesquely in the snow, its windows dark. Somewhere inside, the wealthy bastard was probably nestled beneath the finest linen money could buy, warmed by a crackling fireplace near the foot of his bed.

The tall Southerner burned that image into his mind, refusing to let it go. He vowed that if he managed to escape Gastineau and the imprisonment of the Glory Hole, he would find his way back to St. Michael. And, even if it was with his dying breath, Slocum would make King pay for the trouble he had caused, preferably with the only thing the man owned that could not be replaced with the payment of money. His life.

At the end of the day, as the gray Alaskan sky grew even grayer with the approach of twilight, Henri Gastineau gave the word that ended the party's traveling. They had covered ten miles of rugged terrain since early that morning, pushing both dogs and prisoners to the limits of their stamina. And, in some cases, beyond it.

Two hours after they had started, one of the captives had given out. A lanky farmboy named Drew Hamilton, who had gone to San Francisco on a stock-buying trip, crossed up the frames of his snowshoes and fell flat on his face. The other prisoners had called to Gastineau to stop the sled, but the Canadian merely laughed and cracked his whip loudly, increasing the pace of the dogs. Hamilton had been dragged across the frozen ground for an hour longer, before Gastineau finally stopped the sled to check the canines' harnesses. After that task had been performed, he went back and looked at the last man, tied to the end of his rope. The poor sodbuster was dead, his body torn and bloody from being raked over ice and sharp rocks. When Sean O'Brady suggested digging a grave for the boy, Gastineau laughed uproariously. He explained that a mining drill couldn't penetrate the frozen earth at that time of the year. Then he took his knife, cut Hamilton free from the others, and, without a second thought, ordered the party of sleds to continue on.

Periods of rest were given, but only long enough to enable the captives to drink half-frozen water from a wooden keg and catch their breaths. Then it was back on the trail again, heading ever eastward across the snowy landscape, a landscape that's monotony was interrupted only by stands of pine and spruce, and large outcroppings of snowcapped rock.

Now, after what bad seemed like a torturous eternity on foot, Slocum and the others collapsed in the snow as the sleds crept to a halt. Their feet ached, bruised by walking on the frames of the snowshoes all day, and their legs felt as weak as water. Those who had beards or mustaches now sported dangling masks of crusted ice, their labored breathing having frozen in the sub-zero temperature.

Henri Gastineau stepped from behind his sled and scowled at the men who lay, exhausted, on the ground. "Look at you!" he growled, spitting in disgust. "A poor return for Mr. King's investment, I would say. Why, I have half a mind to draw these pistols and put you weaklings out of your misery. But my boss has paid his money, so it is up to me to make the best of his purchase. But mark my words, you must do much better at the Glory Hole than what you have shown me today. If you fail to do so, I will be forced to kill you."

The men stared up at the bearded Canadian, their eyes burning with hatred. Gastineau seemed only to relish the contempt shown toward him, however. With that roaring laugh of his, he ordered some of the Eskimo guards to gather up fallen branches to build a fire. Then he went to his sled and, unlashing a corner of the canvas cover, began to unload provisions for the evening meal.

A half hour later, both prisoners and captors sat around a roaring fire, huddling before the heat of the flames and eating a bland stew of dried salmon and undercooked rice. Gastineau, Kolabuk, and the other guards ate first, then the sled dogs, and, finally, the thirty-five men who had survived that day's grueling hike across the tundra. King's men washed their grub down with hot coffee, but Slocum and the others were given only a cupful of water from the keg lashed to the back of Kolabuk's sled.

After the meal was over, Slocum sat, shivering in his woolen coat, and listened as Gastineau and his men drank whiskey and talked. At first their conversation included subjects most men discussed while at camp in the wild: moose and deer hunted and brought down by rifle at miraculous distances, whores that had been bedded and the pleasures they had performed, and, of course, gold and hidden fortunes.

When the conversation turned to the journey ahead of them, Slocum listened closely. From what he could gather, they would average ten to twelve miles a day, given that the weather was favorable. Their trek would take them eastward to the Yukon River. Once there, they would take advantage of the frozen waterway, using it as an icy trail northeastward to the settlement of Nulato. After restocking their supplies at the trading post, they would then continue northward to the mountains. Two hundred miles farther on was King's mythical Glory Hole. In all, Gastineau expected their journey to take roughly a month's time, give or take a day or so.

In any event, Slocum knew that their arrival at the gold mine would mean the end of one hell and the beginning of another for those who, like himself, had been abducted and sold into slavery.

As Gastineau and his men laid down Eskimo blankets and heavy robes of bear skin, making their beds for that night, a mournful howl echoed from the direction they had just traveled. It rose in the cold night air, prickling flesh with goose bumps and causing hearts to race.

"What the hell was that?" asked O'Brady, unnerved. "Sounded like a blasted banshee!"

"A wolf," Slocum told him. They listened for a moment. Another cry joined the first one, along with a third. "Make that wolves," he said in correction.

"They must have found the body of the one we left behind," said Kolabuk with a grin of half-rotten teeth. "The one who could not keep up with the rest."

"Yes," agreed a fat Eskimo named Unalla. "And it sounds as if they have feasted upon the poor bastard. Moose and caribou are slim pickings for the wolf this winter. They will eat anything they can drag down or scavage . . . and that means men, as well."

They all listened to the wax and wane of the wolves' savage song for a while, both fascinated and a little frightened by the closeness of the cries. When they faded into silence, Gastineau took a long swallow from the bottle of whiskey, his eyes staring out into the darkness. "Kolabuk . . . you and your men tether the dogs closer to camp," he ordered. "Then gather more wood for the fire. I want it to burn strongly all night."

Kolabuk nodded in understanding. "No need to tempt the beasts," he said, standing and picking three others to join him.

"My thoughts exactly," replied the Canadian in agreement.

As Gastineau's men performed their chores, Slocum lay back on the frozen earth, gathering his warm coat tighter around him. The frigid wind whistled across the lonesome tundra like a train of doom barreling down tracks of ice. But Slocum was too exhausted to care about freezing temperatures or hungry wolves at that moment. He drifted to sleep next to the fire, along with the other captives. Soon, his present troubles were left behind, and he dreamt of whiskey, warm beds, and even warmer women he had known in the past.

8

Four days after their departure from the port of St. Michael, they arrived at the banks of the Yukon River. The waterway originated in the westernmost province of Canada and wound its way through the heart of the Alaska territory to the Bering Sea. When Slocum and his fellow prisoners looked upon the river that cold morning in late December, they found it frozen solid, or at least the upper depths. From where they stood, the Yukon resembled a long trail of gleaming ice bordered on each side by mounds of snow and scraggly stands of pine and fir.

They wasted no time upon their arrival. Henri Gastineau ordered the drivers of the other four sleds to follow his lead, then he cracked his whip and sent his dogs down the steep grade of the Yukon's eastern bank. The animals floundered at first, sinking chest deep into the dense drift of a recent snowfall. But they didn't falter. Before long, they had reached the river's edge. Without hesitation, they leapt onto the snow-encrusted ice and, at Gastineau's command of "Haw!", headed due north.

Slocum expected to find the surface of the river treacherously slick, but that was not the case. The icy top of the Yukon was covered with layers of hard-packed snow, so much so that moving across it felt the same as traveling on solid ground. The only difference was the unnerving sound of the watery currents that echoed from beneath their feet from time to time, reminding them that they were actually traveling above a flowing river.

For the next three days, they traveled northeastward along the Yukon, their pace unrelenting as the miles fell steadily behind them. They deviated from the icy route only at nightfall, shifting to either the western or eastern banks of the river to set up camp. But, come dawn, they were on their way again. They would pause in the center of the river twice a day to rest and eat a cold meal of beef jerky and hardtack, then continue onward.

During the grueling journey, Slocum continued to look for a chance for escape. He thought of Arthur King and the whore named Selana who had orchestrated his abduction, and all that burned through his mind was the desire for vengeance. Several weeks ago, he had arrived in San Francisco, wishing to wait out the winter months gambling and taking it easy. Instead, he had been condemned to spend the next thirty days enduring a death march across a frozen wasteland that he had only heard of and read about.

Perhaps that was what warded off the cold and illness, as well as the progression of grim despair that slowly infected the souls of the others. That fiery need for retribution kept Slocum warm and alert. He knew that if he could only maintain that edge, the right moment would eventually come and he would, indeed, escape. And when he did, he would put his plans for revenge into action, rather than simply think of it every waking hour of every day.

During the seventh day of their trek along the icy trail of the Yukon River, disaster struck, swiftly and without warning.

They were moving up the river at a steady speed, just as they had during the course of a week's time, when a startling noise erupted from the right. At first Slocum thought that it was the sharp crack of a rifle shot ringing through the quiet afternoon air. But it was something much more sinister and deadly for the sled that traveled alongside Henri Gastineau's.

Slocum glanced over in time to see the ice give way beneath the wooden runners of the cargo-laden sled. Its driver—the Eskimo named Unalla—cried out only once before the sled broke through and sank beneath the icy depths of the river that coursed underneath. The currents were strong. They pulled Unalla and the sled beneath the surface quickly, sweeping both man and sleigh into the dark, churning waters.

"Quickly!" yelled Gastineau, directing his men to stop their sleds and prevent any further loss. "Save the dogs and the prisoners! Hurry, before we lose them all!"

Kolabuk and the others rushed toward the widening hole in the ice, but they were too late to save the dog team. Swiftly, the weight of the sinking sled pulled the pack backward. The dogs fought to regain their footing, but the force was too much for them. They yelped and yowled and bit at the harnesses that confined them as, one by one, they were dragged past the jagged edge. Moments later, the cold waters had swallowed all six of the animals, like the dark maw of some hungry beast.

The line of prisoners that was tethered to the sled followed next. With screams of protest and panic, they lost their footing and began to slide toward the edge of the hole. Two men plunged to their watery deaths mere seconds after the last sled dog had dropped beneath the surface. Their pale faces bobbed only once, mouths yearning for air, before they vanished into the merciless currents of the Yukon.

A third man dropped through the icy portal, but remained in limbo for some odd reason, submerged from the waist down. Slocum shifted his attention away from the hole and saw the cause of the captive's salvation. It was in the form of a mass of black muscle and sinew. The giant named Casey Elder was the fourth man in the line, and it was only his colossal strength and presence of mind that saved the entire chain of men from becoming lost. Falling to his back, Elder dug the heels of his snowshoes into the icy crust, halting his slide toward the edge. Then, gripping the rope in both hands, he held fast, saving the third man before he could disappear from view. He attempted to pull backward, perhaps intending to haul the sled and its team from the open hole, but the river was beyond his match in strength and fury. He managed to pull back only a couple of feet of slack, before the rope spun through his grasp, nearly burning through the palms of his heavy leather gloves.

There was a brittle snap as the bowed birch of one of Elder's snowshoes fractured beneath the force that pulled from beyond the watery hole. The Negro attempted to keep his leverage, but it was severely weakened. "Hurry!" he yelled to the guards who ran toward them. "Cut the rope before it takes us all!"

Kolabuk was the first to reach the break in the ice. He regarded the taut length of rope for a moment, then withdrew his Bowie. With a mighty slash, the Eskimo guide brought the gleaming knife downward. Its honed blade parted the rope between Elder and the third man, cleanly and without difficulty. Elder's face was torn between relief and horror as the captive ahead of him was carried, thrashing and screaming, beneath the water by the weight of the dog sled. Soon, nothing was left of the poor man but his hat, which bobbed upon the icy currents like some sort of floating tombstone.

A moment later, Gastineau had slowed his sled, then returned to the scene of the disaster. He glared at the hole in the ice, shaking his head in disgust. "Mr. King will not like this!" he growled. "Six dogs and four men lost! Damn it to hell!"

Slocum saw Gastineau's anger for what it truly was. The bearded man was more concerned with what his boss would say over the loss of dogs and men than with the actual lives of the men themselves. It took a cold-hearted bastard to react that way in the face of such a tragedy, and Gastineau was proving himself to be just that.

The French-Canadian regarded the surviving four who lay on the ice at the edge of the hole. "Split them up and tie them with the others," he ordered. He then glared at the black giant whose strength had saved more than half of the men tied to Unalla's sunken sled. "Do not think that this will buy you any favors when you reach the Glory Hole, Elder," said Gastineau. "You will be treated the same as all the others who work there. Now, get up!"

Casey Elder's eyes burned like dark coals as he slowly rose to his feet. For a moment, Slocum was certain that the big Negro would reach out and, closing his massive fist around Gastineau's throat, throttle the Canadian before anyone else could react. But, fortunately for him, Elder stayed his hand. He said nothing as Gastineau turned and stomped back to his sled.

After the four prisoners had been divided and tied to the ropes of the surviving four sleds, they were on their way again. They continued northward, all ears alert for the telltale crack of thin ice shattering beneath the stress of too much weight. But it did not come a second time that day. They drove onward, leaving the hole in the ice as a grim memorial to those who had been sucked into the dark and treacherous depths of the Yukon River.

9

A week passed. The month of December gave way to January, but the only indication that such a change had taken place was the counting of the days in Slocum's head. It was difficult to keep track of such things. The hunger for decent food, the intense cold, and the sheer exhaustion that followed each day's travel only dulled a man's thoughts. Things like time and comfort were forgotten in order to concentrate on more important matters like survival and making it through another day alive. But, even though Slocum endured the same grueling pace and inhumane conditions as his fellow captives, he tried hard to prevent it from affecting him mentally. The rage he carried inside kept his thoughts sharp and nimble, even if his body and stamina weren't quite as lucky.

Seventy miles north from the point where they had begun their journey along the frozen Yukon, Henri Gastineau decided that it would be safer if they deviated from their original route. More and more, they began to come across hazardous spots in the ice. Several times, they found large holes in the surface where an unsuspecting moose or caribou had fallen through and drowned in the freezing water.

Not wanting to lose any more of Arthur King's workers to the river's treacherous currents, Gastineau returned to the riverbank on the Yukon's eastern side. The four sleds continued onward, riding the heavy drifts at a slower pace.

The flat and relatively smooth surface of the frozen river had proven to be a much quicker route in comparison to the thick snowbanks and jagged outcroppings of rock that the dog sleds were now forced to contend with.

One thing that Slocum found difficult to deal with was the complete silence that the Alaskan landscape seemed to possess. Slocum had ridden through lonely mountain passes and across barren desert in his time, but nowhere he had ever traveled before had been as utterly quiet as the country he now found himself in. It was a silence as noiseless as the snow was white, a hush so total that it was almost unnatural. True, there was the sound of panting dogs, the cracks of the sledmen's whips, and the thudding of the prisoners' weary footfalls in the snow, but other than that there was nothing. The stillness hung throughout the valleys and ravines like a tangible presence, almost oppressively so.

Three days from the settlement of Nulato, they again encountered trouble.

The dogs that pulled the four sleds were seasoned animals. They had made the trip from St. Michael to the Glory Hole numerous times in the past. But their collective experience didn't insulate them against the problems the rugged terrain threw their way. Sometimes the drifts were so deep that they sank into the snow up to their backs. They floundered and fought to pull free, and, in turn, Gastineau had to delay their journey in order to untangle the teams' harnesses. Other times, the dogs caught the scent of wolves while traveling through a narrow pass and grew frightened, reluctant to press on. That was when the drivers were forced to use their whips more urgently. The tips bit fur and flesh, rather than the cold winter air, and, more afraid of their masters' punishment than their bestial kin, the dogs would continue on.

One such mishap took place as they left a flat valley and entered a stand of dense spruce. The team that pulled Gastineau's sled was steadily making its way through the forest, when something darted across their path. It was an adult porcupine the size of full-grown cat. The lead dog of the team was caught off guard. Out of instinct rather than good judgment, the canine leapt at the porcupine, landing upon its back with all four feet. A second later, it knew the error of its actions. A scuffle erupted between dog and rodent. The two rolled around in the snow for a moment, accompanied by the most ferocious hissing and agonizing yowling that Slocum had ever heard before. An instant later, the porcupine had escaped into the woods, leaving Gastineau's lead dog with a lasting impression that was, unfortunately, a fatal one.

With a curse on his lips, Gastineau jumped from the back of the sled and ran to the front of the team. The other dogs merely stood there, whimpering, confused over what had happened to their leader. The dog lay on its side in the bloody snow, writhing in pain. Long quills protruded from the animal's head and snout, as well as its chest, back, stomach, and legs.

"Dammit!" said Gastineau as he stood over the wounded dog. "The mutt has been skewered!"

The drivers of the other sleds had stopped their teams, and they, too, watched as the dog yowled in agony. They all knew that nothing could be done for the animal. Already some of the porcupine quills had begun to work their way into the dog's body, spearing past skin and muscle and puncturing its internal organs. The canine would likely lie there and suffer several hours before it finally died.

With an angry growl of disgust, Henri Gastineau drew the Remington .44 from the sash of his coat. He cocked the revolver and, lowering its muzzle to the back of the dog's head, fired. Blood and brains painted the Alaskan snow as the animal was mercilessly put out of its misery.

For a moment, Gastineau stood there, staring down at the twitching body of the lead dog. Then his dark mood seemed to lighten and he smiled. Slocum could tell by that smile that the bearded Canadian was up to no good.

Gastineau stalked past the other dogs and the sled they were harnessed to. He walked down the line of shackled men, his eyes fixed on a particular one. Slocum thought that he was looking at him at first, but he was mistaken. Gastineau passed right by him and, withdrawing a key from his pocket, began to unlock the cuffs of the man behind him—Tex McCoy.

Soon, the Canadian had the lanky Texan by the collar of his coat, dragging him toward the front of the sled. "Come with me, cowboy," he said with a sneer. "You will be my lead dog for the next few days."

The thought of his injured friend having to serve in such a degrading manner was simply too much for Slocum. "Take me, Gastineau!" he yelled out. "Leave him alone and I'll do it for you."

"Shut up!" growled Gastineau over his shoulder. With a brawny arm, he shoved Tex to the ground next to the dead dog. "Take off his harness and put it on yourself. Do it now!"

Puzzled, the cowboy with the fractured skull stared at the dog. Its legs were already beginning to stiffen, and steam rose from the ugly crater in the back of its head. Then Tex turned his head and, suddenly, a familiar fire blazed in his eyes. Slocum could see it from where he stood—the defiance of a man who had braved cattle rustlers, hostile Indians, and everything that Mother Nature could throw at him with both hands.

"No," he said.

That's right, Tex, thought Slocum. *Come back to your senses.*

Gastineau stared at the cowpoke as if he couldn't believe his ears. "What did you say to me?"

"I said you can go straight to hell," McCoy said flatly, his eyes no longer dull and confused.

The Canadian regarded the cowboy for a long moment, then shrugged his broad shoulders. "Very well," he said. "If you refuse, then you are about as useful to me as the dog."

Slocum knew what was coming before it actually happened. Gastineau turned and gave Slocum a toothy grin. Then he stuck the Remington back into his sash and withdrew the Colt Navy.

"No!" yelled Slocum. "Damn you, Gastineau . . . don't do it!"

The bearded man merely laughed in reply. Before the tall Georgian could utter another word of protest, the .36 pistol had been lowered and its hammer cocked. The silence of the Alaskan wilderness was filled with thunder as the gun went off, releasing a flash of fire, smoke, and rounded lead. Slocum watched in horror as an ugly hole appeared between Tex's eyes and he slumped forward in the snow. Unlike the dog, McCoy failed even to jerk or twitch. He was stone-cold dead before he even hit the ground.

With a swagger, Henri Gastineau left the front of the dog team and walked back to where Slocum stood. The dark-haired Georgian wanted to launch himself at the man and choke the bastard to death with the chains of his shackles, but he was smart enough to fight down the urge to act on his impulse. Slocum's eyes blazed with hatred, and his jaw was firmly set as the Canadian approached him, gun in hand.

"Come with me, Slocum," he said with a sadistic grin. "You wanted to take your friend's place so badly, now is your chance."

"I'm going to kill you," the Southerner said in a low voice that only Gastineau could hear.

The Canadian chuckled. "Perhaps later, but not today," he told him. "No, today you will be my dog instead." And, with that, he cautiously separated Slocum from the others and marched him to the front of the sled.

Slocum stood there for a moment. He stared down at the man he had once shared a Texas cattle drive with. There were few men that Slocum considered to be friends. Tex McCoy had been one of the rare ones. For a blinding instant, Slocum's grief turned into full-blown madness. He nearly turned and attacked the grinning Canadian. But before he could lose his senses entirely, he quelled the murderous desire for retribution. He knew that if he made one wrong move toward Gastineau, it would only bring a lethal shot from his own gun. And Slocum had too much at stake—too much to make right eventually—to allow himself to grow careless in the face of the cold-blooded foreman.

"Put the harness on," demanded Gastineau. He cocked the hammer, turning the Colt's engraved cylinder to its next loaded chamber. "Do it . . . or I will kill you like I did the cowboy."

Slocum looked back toward the men he had been confined with. Sean O'Brady stared back at him, his eyes hard, yet urging him to do as Gastineau said. O'Brady was a proud man himself, but he was smart enough to know when a man was bluffing. And he knew that, at that moment, Henri Gastineau was deadly serious.

Slowly, Slocum turned to the two bodies that lay at his feet. He stepped over Tex and, crouching next to the carcass of the dog, began to unbuckle its harness. It took him a few minutes of fumbling and tightening, but, finally, the straps of tanned leather were securely bound around his chest and shoulders.

Gastineau roared with laughter. "Look!" he called to Kolabuk and the others. "Look at my fine new dog!" The Eskimo and his fellow guards joined in the laughter, finding great humor in Slocum's humiliation.

The tall Southerner turned and looked back at the other prisoners. None of them shared in their captors' laughter. Instead, their faces were grim and sad. Sean O'Brady glanced away, unable to look Slocum in the eyes.

The weight of shame threatened to pull down the Georgian's spirit, but he refused to let it. Instead, he focused on the trail ahead. All that mattered to him at that moment was to stay alive long enough to pay Gastineau back for killing Tex and subjecting him to the humiliating position he was now in. And he vowed that when the time came, he would show Gastineau about as much mercy as the evil Canadian had shown the injured cowboy from San Antonio.

It wasn't long before Gastineau was back at the rear of the sled. Smiling cruelly, he unfurled his whip and, with a sharp snap, sent the length of braided leather whirling close to Slocum's head. The tip nicked the Southerner's right ear, cutting it shallowly and drawing blood. Slocum refused to cry out in pain, however. He suffered the wound in silence and, straining against his harness, began to move forward.

"Mush!" roared Gastineau with a laugh. "Mush, I say!"

Slocum did as he was told. He blocked out the Canadian's laughter and, increasing his pace, began to set out across the snowy landscape. The other five dogs didn't know what to think at first and shied from following his lead. But they didn't hesitate for long. A few cracks from their master's whip changed their opinion of their new leader. Soon, the sled was moving steadily along the eastern bank of the Yukon River, heading northward.

10

They arrived at the settlement of Nulato in late evening.
Very little could be seen of the town in the gathering dusk.
There were a dozen crude dwellings constructed of cut sap-
lings and tanned elk skins—the homes of an Eskimo tribe,
or what was left of one. Standing in a circular courtyard in
the center of the shelters was a totem pole perhaps ten or
twelve feet in height, sporting the carved and painted faces
of six of the tribe's most fierce and feared gods. A single
fire burned a few feet from the totem, but no one was there
to benefit from it. Apparently, it was there to ward off wild
animals, rather than provide warmth or heat for cooking.

Fifty yards from the Eskimo village stood a single building—the only civilized-looking structure in the entire settlement. It was low and long and built of sturdy logs and
mud chinking, and its pitched roof was covered with cedar
shingles. A lean-to stood to the left side of the building,
housing a blacksmith's shop and half a dozen stables for
horses. To the right stood a kennel that held twenty or more
sled dogs of various breeds, as well as an outhouse.

As they made their way down a steep ridge and approached
the village, Henri Gastineau hauled back on the reins and
yelled "Whoa!" In response, the team of his sled, with
Slocum at the head, slowed to a gradual stop. The tall
Southerner rested for the first time in two hours, his hands
on his knees and his breathing labored. He felt the dog

behind him move closer, sniffing at his legs, smelling the odor of his sweat, along with the scent of his anger.

Slocum heard the crunch of the Canadian's footsteps in the deep snow. Soon, the man stood directly next to him. The Georgian's temper flared. He would have probably made some foolish move toward Gastineau if he hadn't been so exhausted. For the past three days, Slocum had acted as Gastineau's lead dog. Through dense drifts and thick stands of timber, he had guided the sled and its canine team. He had fallen in his tracks several times along the way, his stamina giving out after miles of bearing the lion's share of the labor. Only Gastineau's degrading taunts and numerous lashes from the tip of his whip kept Slocum going. The Southerner had felt the sting of a whip before, several times in the past, and it was one sensation that he truly hated. Both his flesh and his mind held the scars of past tortures. His skin had healed from the wounds, but his thoughts still ached in memory of those sadistic hands that wielded braided leather and knew how put it to its most effective use.

He felt the whip at that moment as he leaned forward in exhaustion, but there was no pain to its touch. No, it came as a teasing at the nape of his neck, bringing an emotion much worse than fear and agony. Slocum felt a shudder of rage quake throughout him as the length of the whip caressed his flesh.

"Unharness yourself, Slocum," instructed Gastineau, his voice full of smug humor. "You've been a good dog these past few days, but I prefer the kind with four paws and a tail. They stink much less than you do."

Gastineau's men laughed at their boss's lame joke, but Slocum said nothing in reply. He simply worked at the harness that had imprisoned him for three days, then cast it away. He had some difficulty in lifting his arms above his chest. His shoulders and back ached from the strain of tugging the sled for such a great distance, even though the dogs had carried some of the load. Also his armpits were chafed and raw where the leather straps of the harness had rubbed at the skin beneath his clothing, raising painful blisters.

Slocum felt the cold muzzle of a revolver—perhaps his own Colt Navy—press against the back of his neck, prodding him toward the line of captives who were tied to the rear of the sled. Wearily, he allowed Gastineau to march him back to the place where he had been confined before. He was shackled, then fastened to the length of heavy rope. Then the gun was removed from his neck, and Gastineau stepped away, grinning broadly amid his tangle of red whiskers. He stared at the Southerner, as if waiting for him to speak out in anger. But when Slocum refused to utter a single word, the Canadian turned and, laughing, walked toward the log structure. "Untie them and bring them inside," he called to his men.

Gastineau's order was obeyed. Soon, the prisoners were marched, single file, past the covered smithy, to the front doorway of the building. A crudely painted sign that hung over the door read: "BOYD'S TRADING POST—LIQUOR, FOOD, SUPPLIES, & WHORES—MONTGOMERY BOYD, PROPRIETOR."

Once through the entrance, Slocum was greeted with familiar scents and sounds—the smell of tobacco smoke, whiskey, and unwashed bodies, as well as the clink of bottle necks on shot glasses and the tittering laughter of drunken whores. It took Slocum's eyes a moment to adjust to the glow of seal-oil lamps, which hung from every other rafter of the low-slung ceiling. When they finally did, he saw the interior of the trading post for what it was. One side served as a saloon of sorts. A couple of bearded fur trappers sat at one of four crude tables, fondling a couple of Eskimo women and drinking home-brewed hoochinoo, a foul-tasting liquor brewed from bark, berries, molasses, and yeast. The bar was made up of a long board positioned between two barrels, with a shelf of bottles and flasks hanging on the wall behind it. Rusted lard cans sat around the sawdust-covered floor, serving as makeshift spittoons. Next to the bar stood a potbelly stove stoked hot with kindling and coal, and to the far side of it was a general store. All manner of supplies, mining equipment, and canned food was arranged on shelves that lined every inch of available wall space.

"Monty, you old polecat you!" roared Gastineau as he unbuckled his snowshoes and crossed the floor, his hand outstretched.

A fat man in a shirt of checkered flannel and suspendered britches stood behind the bar. He possessed a head of thinning gray hair and a thick handlebar mustache of the same light hue. He also possessed an amazing array of knife scars across his forehead, nose, and jawline, and Slocum saw two evenly spaced bullet holes, one beneath each cheekbone, as if a bullet had passed through one side of the man's face and out the other.

"Gastineau, you ornery son of a bitch!" greeted Monty Boyd. The owner of the trading post shook the Canadian's hand firmly. "What're you doing back in this neck of the woods?"

"Taking some workers up to the Glory Hole," said Gastineau. "Mr. King likes his mine to remain on schedule. It is hard to keep it running with so many dying of consumption, fever, and lead poisoning." He patted the stock of his rifle.

Monty nodded his gray head. "It is hard to find good help these days," he said. He eyed the shackled men that

had been assembled along the walls of the trading post.
"Pretty shabby crew you've got there. Half of 'em look
like their arms would pop out the sockets if they tried to
lift a nine-pound hammer. But some of them will likely do
the job well enough. That big nigger there, for example.
He'll do the work of three men alone, if kept in line."

"Oh, we'll see to that," assured Gastineau with a grin.
"How about a drink to thaw me out? And some grub for
these men, as sorry as they may be."

"Coming right up," said Monty. He handed Gastineau a
jug of hooch, then turned to an elderly Eskimo woman who
crouched next to the stove. "Rustle up a kettle of beans and
salt pork for these men. And put on a bear steak for my
friend here. The biggest one we have."

As Boyd's squaw went to work, the two men shared a
drink from the jug. "Where's Kolabuk?" asked Monty. "Did
he join you on this trip?"

"He's outside tending to the dogs," said Gastineau. "He
should be in shortly."

It was at that moment that Slocum noticed something.
At the mention of Kolabuk's name, the two trappers at
the table traded glances. From the malice in their eyes,
he figured that both held some sort of grudge against the
big Eskimo. Slocum watched as they quietly shooed the
two whores away and sat there, facing the front door. He
noticed that their long-arms were close at hand. One was
a big-bore Hawken rifle decorated with fancy brasswork,
while the other was a Winchester carbine with rabbit fur
tied over the stock and foregrip.

"I lost a dog a while back," said Gastineau. "My lead
dog, in fact. Would you have another to trade?"

Monty Boyd took a long swig of the homemade hooch
and winced as it burned its way down into his belly. "Yes,
sir, I do believe I have one in the kennel for you. A big

white malamute a feller from Fairbanks traded me a couple months ago. And you won't even have to train him. He's led his share of teams in his time." Monty eyed Gastineau slyly. "So, what do you have to trade?"

Slocum felt his blood begin to boil when the Canadian reached toward the the sash of his coat. But, fortunately, he did not draw the Colt Navy. Instead, Gastineau laid McCoy's .44 Remington on the top of the crude drinking bar. "How about this?"

Monty picked up the revolver and inspected it with interest. "Nice gun. I always wanted me a hogleg cannon like this. Don't look to be more than a couple years old, either." He extended the pistol at arm's length and worked the hammer several times, testing the smoothness of its action.

"You get one of the Eskimos to carve you some whalebone grips and etch them up right fancy, and you'll have a showpiece the envy of every man in the territory," said Gastineau.

The owner of Nulato's only trading post seemed to like the idea. "All right," he said. Monty spat into his palm and shook the Canadian's hand. "It's a deal!"

Boyd and Gastineau were having another drink to finalize the trade, when the door opened with a gust of icy air. Everyone looked toward the one who entered. Kolabuk stepped through the doorway, stooping slightly to keep his head from hitting the top of the frame. Slocum watched as he shucked his gloves and then glanced around the dimly lit drinking parlor. The moment he saw the two trappers sitting at the table, a sparkle came to his dark eyes. The Eskimo smiled in a way that seemed more reptilian than human, then lifted his right arm. Fisted in his brown hand was the big Sharps rifle.

Events happened fast and furious after that. One of the trappers grabbed at his Hawken and even had the iron hammer cocked, but still he was much too slow. Kolabuk's Sharps boomed like a thundercloud, filling the room with gunsmoke. The rifle's heavy-grain slug tore into the center of the trapper's chest, knocking him back in his chair. The man toppled over as the bullet exited between his shoulder blades, painting the log wall of the trading post with blood.

The other fared a little better, but not much. He at least got his Winchester to his shoulder and levered off a shot. The bullet went wide, though, striking the door frame a few inches from Kolabuk's head. The big Eskimo merely laughed at the man and, discarding the Sharps, withdrew the long-bladed Bowie. Kolabuk's arm was a blur as he sent the knife spinning across the room. The weapon found its mark before the trapper could fire a second time. It buried itself up to the hilt in the left side of the man's buckskin jacket. The Winchester clattered to the saloon floor, and the trapper stood there, weaving on his feet for a moment, before his eyes rolled up into his head and he joined his partner in death.

All eyes watched as Kolabuk grunted to himself, then crossed the saloon to where the two men laid. The Eskimo yanked his Bowie from the chest of his last victim, wiped the blood from the blade on the fringed sleeve of the trapper's coat, then returned it to its beaded sheath. After that, he took a lengthy swallow from the jug the two men had shared and, crouching, began to search the bodies for valuables.

Monty Boyd and Henri Gastineau turned back to their own drinking. "I always wondered what would happen when the Turner Brothers crossed paths with ol' Kolabuk again. They never did forgive him for killing their daddy in that poker game down at Otter Creek."

"I knew he'd get the best of them," said Gastineau. "Kolabuk is faster than the strike of a rattler, with gun or knife. It was no contest, in my opinion."

Monty nodded in agreement, then turned back to his squaw. "Throw another steak on the griddle for Kolabuk here. Then drag these carcasses outside and scrub that mess off the wall over yonder. It's enough to ruin a man's appetite."

The Eskimo woman regarded the chores ahead of her and scowled. Then she slapped another bear steak on the stove and turned her attention back to her cooking.

11

They left Boyd's Trading Post and the settlement of Nulato the following morning. From what little Slocum overheard, he gathered that two hundred miles of treacherous wilderness lay ahead of them. They lashed as many supplies as possible to the four sleds, harnessed the new dog to the front of Gastineau's team, then started northeastward, splitting from the fork of the Yukon and traveling along the winding channel of the Koyukuk River.

If the captives thought the worst of the journey was behind them, they were sorely mistaken. If anything, the terrain past Nulato was twice as rugged as that which they had already covered, nearly impassable in places. Snowdrifts stood six feet deep in some spots, and there were stands of timber so dense that the dogsleds could not find a clear way through. They ended up traveling miles from their original route, merely to find a safe way past those obstacles. Gastineau tried using the frozen Koyukuk the same way they had used the Yukon at the start of their journey, but it proved to be even more hazardous. They were on the river only a day when they encountered half a dozen dangerous spots in the ice. Near late evening of their eighth day from Nulato, they witnessed a small herd of moose attempting to cross the frozen river ahead of them. The icy crust gave way beneath their weight, and they disappeared beneath the surface, bellowing wildly as the cold undertow of the Koyukuk dragged them from view. Gastineau and Kolabuk decided then that their new route wasn't worth the risk. They camped on the eastern bank of the river that night, then set off across solid ground the following morning.

As the days turned into weeks, more of the prisoners were lost to the cruelty of the elements. One fell victim to pneumonia and died choking on the mucus that clogged his lungs. And as the party traveled through a particularly narrow pass, snow dislodged from the steep walls, causing a small but deadly avalanche. Fortunately, the slide hit only the last sled of the expedition, claiming only three of the captives, at the end of the line. The men were buried beneath tons of snow, ice, and rock, so quickly that they had no time to cry out in alarm. Rather than dig them out, the driver of the sled simply cut the rope and continued onward, leaving their bodies in the icy grave.

Since they left the town of St. Michael, the number of King's gold slaves had dropped from thirty-six to twenty-seven. At night, when they were huddled around the blaze of a roaring camp fire, Slocum and O'Brady talked in low voices. They knew that escape was necessary for their survival. Even if the party reached King's Glory Hole without any further casualties, there were sure to be others after their arrival. From the way Gastineau and Kolabuk talked about the gold mine, they knew that it would prove to be a hell on earth. From what they could gather, several dozen workers had died in one way or another during the past year. Some had fallen to disease and consumption, while others had died due to cave-ins and faulty charges of blasting powder. Some had fallen short of their captors' expectations and were cold-bloodedly executed, either because they were too exhausted to toil in the mine or because they had attempted to escape.

Slocum and O'Brady were careful with their secret discussion, however. They knew that if they mentioned their plans to the wrong person, it could prove to be their downfall. Most of the captives had been pushed to the limit of physical and mental endurance. They didn't possess the patience to wait for the right time and place to make the escape. They were so filled with desperation that they would likely try to flee at the first opportunity, whether it was a good one or not. The Southerner and the Irishman were aware that the deck was stacked against them. Although the prisoners outnumbered Gastineau's men three to one, there was still the sobering fact that the guards were well armed and willing to put their guns to quick use. There was also the fact the Slocum and the others were shackled at the wrists at all times, restricting their movements severely. Even if they did escape from Gastineau's party and into the Alaskan wilderness, they would still be doomed. There was no way a man could survive in such a hostile land with his hands linked by twelve inches of sturdy iron chain.

There was also the problem of wolves to contend with. Since leaving Nulato, they had been followed by a pack of timber wolves, roughly eight to ten in number. The Alaskan winter had, so far, been a particularly cruel one, and the pack's food supply was, unfortunately, scarce. During the entire trip, Slocum and the others had seen only a few deer and caribou along the way, half the number that normally would have been there. Kolabuk attributed it to the heavy snowfall. The big game had migrated south in search of leaves and grass, leaving the wolves behind to fend for themselves the best they could. That, in turn, turned the beasts mean and hungry. They would attack anything they could if given half the chance. Gastineau and the others had to keep rifles at the ready and camp fires stoked hot and bright in order to keep the scavengers at bay.

Slocum knew that it would be his best bet to wait until he reached the Glory Hole to attempt an escape. Then, he would be better able to equip himself with a gun and provisions before he set off across the frozen tundra. He was certain that his chances for survival would be pretty slim if he braved weather and wolves with nothing to fight back with.

It was nearly the end of the month of January when Gastineau and his cargo of slaves finally reached their destination.

The snowy plains of the Koyukuk River Valley gradually rose, giving way to a range of lofty mountains that stretched from east to west as far as the eye could see. As they traveled into the bosom of the range, Slocum was amazed at how utterly barren the place was. The tops of the mountains were capped with snow, but the sheer sides of the peaks were almost naked stone and earth. Vegetation was sparce. Dwarf willows and small stands of white spruce clung to the mountainsides, but that was all. A low mist hung close to the ground, choking the broad passes with dense fog in early morning and late evening. All and all, the mountains of northern Alaska seemed, to Slocum, to be the most forlorn and godforsaken place on the face of the earth.

Four days after they entered the range, they arrived at the mine owned by Arthur King. It was not much to look at—simply a bunkhouse and a few rickety outbuildings standing on a grade a few hundred yards up the face of the range's tallest peak. Next to the bunkhouse gaped the mouth of a mine shaft supported by sturdy timber. From the opening snaked a pair of iron rails with tarred ties set underneath them—tracks for the ore cars to travel on. Next to the mine stood several large bins constructed of heavy lumber. Although the heaps that rested within the bins were covered with canvas tarps, Slocum saw the hint of yellow metal peeking from beneath the folds. Apparently, the harvests of gold that were mined during the winter months were deposited there, where they awaited transportation back to St. Michael by barge when the Koyukuk and Yukon rivers thawed out come springtime.

When the sleds and their human cargo arrived in the center of the mining camp that January afternoon, Gastineau drew the Colt Navy from his sash and fired once into the air. A moment later, a lanky, rawboned man with a nose as crooked as a pump spigot opened the door of the bunkhouse and stepped out into the cold, holding a ten-gauge Parker in both hands. When he saw who had fired the shot, he lowered his shotgun and spat a stream of tobacco juice into the snow. "Damn you, Gastineau!" grumbled the fellow. "You just about scared the shit outta me!"

The Canadian laughed. "It is good to see you again, too, Finch," he said.

The man named Finch eyed the men who were tied to the backs of the four dog sleds. "I see you got 'em. Not as many as I expected, though."

"We lost a few along the way," Gastineau explained. "But they should help pick up production quite a bit."

"And about time!" said Finch. "We've lost five more ourselves since you left. We're down to a quarter ton of ore per week."

"That won't do. Mr. King will have our hides if we don't pick up the pace and deliver our quota by early April."

"I'll say!" Finch glanced over at Gastineau's sled and the bulk of the provisions lashed to the back of it. "What'd you bring? Whiskey, I hope. I've had to brew my own from willow root, coffee grounds, and powdered moose antler . . .

and you know how dadblamed awful that tastes!"

"I've brought six jugs of hoochinoo, courtesy of our friend Monty Boyd," said Gastineau. "Salt pork, beans, sugar, and salt, too."

Finch licked his whiskered lips. "We ran outta all of them last month. Don't have any whores hidden in there with the supplies somewhere, do you?"

Gastineau chuckled. "Sorry, Finch. But I did come away from Boyd's with a new sled dog, if you want to try your luck with it."

"Real funny, Henri!" grumbled Finch. Then he walked out to the sled to help unload the provisions.

Gastineau ordered Kolabuk and the rest of his men to untie the captives and assemble them near the opening of the mine. Within a few minutes, all twenty-seven stood at the entrance, staring at the pitch darkness that stretched within. "All right, you men, listen up!" said the French-Canadian. "You are now about to enter the fabled Glory Hole, called such because so many have been sent on the road to glory mining its wealth. I suggest you take a long look around, because for some of you, it will be your last glimpse of the outside world. Some of you who behave yourselves and do a good day's work may earn the privilege of toting the ore to the ground level and dumping it in those bins over there. Most of you, however, will probably disappoint me and, in turn, will likely never see the light of day again."

The men stood there in stunned silence, the magnitude of their slavery finally sinking in. Slocum didn't allow the grim prospect of imprisonment underground to phase him, though. He promised himself that he would reach the outside world and be a free man once again. It might take him a while to accomplish that goal, but he would do it— or die trying.

"Just remember what Mr. King told you several weeks ago and you'll do okay," reminded Gastineau. "But forget his warning, and you may very well end up with a bullet in your brainpan. Or, even worse, stripped naked and cast into the wilderness to freeze to death."

Slocum stared the man in the eyes and sensed that he wasn't joking about his last threat. Gastineau was just mean enough to do such a thing.

"You heard him!" said Kolabuk in that thundering voice of his. "Now, into the mine. And watch your heads. We wouldn't want you to bash your brains out, now would we?"

Slocum heard Gastineau's laughter echo from behind as he and the other twenty-six were marched into the dark gullet of the mine. They turned a corner in the tunnel and suddenly came upon a section lit by seal-oil lanterns that hung from spikes in the walls. As they walked, Slocum studied the walls of the passageway. No evidence of precious metal showed on that level. Only solid granite and clusters of quartz could be seen, along with the occasional timber wedged there to reenforce the tunnel against the weight of the mountain above. Apparently, the mother lode was located in one of the lower levels of the mine. How many levels to the complex there actually were, Slocum could only guess at.

A hundred feet into the tunnel, it abruptly came to an end. Or, rather, it turned into a shaft that plunged into the depths of the earth. They were divided into groups of five, then the first group was herded into the iron-and-wood cage of a crude freight elevator. Several men, including Casey Elder, were put to work at a massive winch that took the cage from level to level and then back to the surface again.

Slocum was one of the first who took the trip down the shaft. As the cage made its way into the belly of the mine, the Georgian began to glimpse traces of color in the walls. At first, they appeared only as spots of gold, then, farther down, entire veins of the gleaming metal started to show. Slocum began to count off each level as they passed by. When they reached the seventh level, the cage jerked to creaking halt and they were herded off. Then the elevator ascended to the surface to fetch the next group of prisoners.

Eventually, some of Gastineau's men took their places at the winch, and the rest of the slaves found themselves in the tunnel of the seventh level. With rifle barrels proding at their backs, the twenty-seven made their way down the corridor, until they reached the heart of Arthur King's Glory Hole.

It turned out to be far from what Slocum had expected. Instead of a network of interconnecting tunnels and shafts, the Glory Hole was a huge cavern perhaps eighty feet high and twice that distance in length and width. Men in chains worked at the walls of the cave with sledgehammers and pickaxes, tackling massive veins of gold that were three and four feet wide in places. The veteran laborers of the Glory Hole regarded the new prisoners only fleetingly before turning their attention back to their work. From the fear in their hollow eyes, Slocum could tell that they knew better than to slack from their pace, even for a short period of time.

One thing that drew Slocum's interest was a natural waterfall that poured endlessly from a crevice in the ceiling of the cavern and ran down the back wall into a circular pool. From the warmth within the cave, he could tell that the water originated from a hot spring that coursed beneath the frozen surface of the Alaskan mountains. Exactly how such a phenomenon could exist in such a place, Slocum couldn't hope to explain.

"This is it," said Gastineau. "Home sweet home for the rest of your miserable lives. You get to rest for the remainder of the day. But tomorrow you work—all of you. And you'd best keep up with the pace of the others. I expect our quota of gold to double by the end of the week, then triple the week after that."

After Gastineau had left the cavern, heading back to the elevator that would take him to the uppermost level, Slocum and the others settled on the floor of the cave near a far wall. The Southerner had been correct in his assessment of the natural spring. The temperature of the cavern was so warm that they ended up having to remove their heavy coats. It wasn't long before the humidity of the chamber raised a sweat on them all, although none of them had yet lifted a single finger in labor.

"We've got to get out of this place," said Sean O'Brady in a low voice. "If we don't, it'll surely be the death of us. I'm certain of it."

"Don't worry," Slocum assured him. "We'll get out of here . . . when the time is right. But not a moment before. If we get impatient, we could both end up like poor Tex."

O'Brady remembered the lanky Texan's cruel murder and nodded. "I understand. But, Lord Almighty on high, I hope the chance comes soon."

"So do I," replied Slocum. One look at the hell around them made him realize that escape from the Glory Hole was, truly, a matter of life and death.

12

The next day, Slocum was subjected to the most grueling day of labor in his life.

Not that the tall Southerner was a stranger to hard work. He had been raised on a Georgia farm where a day's chores began at dawn and ended well past dusk. Even after he had crossed the Mississippi and wandered west, he had done his fair share of cow punching, mule skinning, and coal mining. But no job he had ever held could compare to the work he was forced to do that day in the dark pit of Arthur King's Glory Hole.

At five in the morning, he and the other new arrivals were rudely roused from their sleep, and, just as in the hold of Shanghai Kelly's ship, their ankles were locked in shackles of heavy iron. Only eighteen inches of chain linked their feet together, minimizing their freedom of movement. The bonds limited them to a pigeon-toed walk and nothing more. If any of them attempted to run, he would fall flat on his face before he traveled ten feet.

After they had been fed a quick breakfast of bitter coffee and rancid oatmeal, they joined the legion who had been working the gold mine upon their arrival. From what Slocum saw, there were forty more who had suffered the same fate as they had. All were powerful, able-bodied men, except for a few who were slight of build and one who looked to be past the age of seventy. They regarded

Slocum and the others with flat, emotionless stares, almost as if they weren't there.

Henri Gastineau himself served as that day's foreman. He split the sixty-seven men into ten teams, then assigned each team a specific task. The crew that Slocum joined had the difficult job of excavating a gold vein that was roughly fifteen feet in length and three feet in width. Soon, he found a nine-pound sledgehammer fisted in his hands. He went to work on the vein at an even pace, neglecting to go at the wall full-force as some of the others did. Slocum wasn't an hour into the excavation when the muscles of his arms and back began to ache, growing ponderously heavy with the strain of continuous hammerstrikes. Some men collapsed in exhaustion, unable to raise their arms, let alone the weight of their hammers. But, while they were forced back to work by curses and lashes from Gastineau's whip, Slocum merely shed his shirt and, muscles glistening with sweat, continued to batter away at the vein in the wall with slow, but powerful blows.

By the time they stopped for dinner eight hours later, Slocum too was feeling exhausted from their morning's labor. Even after he laid his hammer aside and choked down a meal of lukewarm water and dry corn pone, his muscles still hurt, thrumming painfully every few seconds, as if still absorbing the shock of the sledge against stone. Then, twenty minutes later, the men were back to work again.

Sixteen hours after they had first begun, Gastineau gave the order to cease. The racket of picks and hammers against rock stopped, and only the distant roar of the underground waterfall filled the cavern. The veteran slaves of the Glory Hole tossed down their tools, then made their way slowly to the warm spring. They shed their clothing and showered in the cascading water, washing away a day's worth of sweat and grit. Slocum and the other newcomers were not up to

following their example, though. Exhausted, they slumped
to the ground next to the wall where they had labored,
breathing deeply and allowing taut and aching muscles to
relax. Even when Gastineau and his men came around with
the last meal of the day, some of them lacked the strength
to get up. Slocum, however, forced himself to his feet and
joined the line for his share of weak tea and beans. He knew
he must eat and keep up his strength if he were ever going
to make it out that hellhole alive.

An hour after supper, Slocum and O'Brady were sitting
against a wall of the massive cave, when a lean and spidery
form approached them from out the gloom of the seal-oil
lamps. A moment later, they recognized their visitor as the
elderly worker they had seen earlier that day. He was clad
in dirty, threadbare britches held up with suspenders, filthy
red longjohns, and mule-eared boots that looked as if their
soles were worn plumb down to the cobbler nails. The old
man was bald, but possessed a tangled wreath of sooty gray
whiskers, and a mouth that held only a few remaining teeth.

"Howdy!" said the elderly fellow, eyeing the dark-haired
Southerner and the redheaded Irishman. "Pardon the intru-
sion, but you look like a couple of fellers who still have
their wits about them. Mind if I join you?"

Slocum studied the old man, at first suspicious of his
bold introduction. Then he saw him for what he was—
someone who had survived the trials of the Glory Hole
and, in turn, was eager to talk to those who were equally
strong of spirit. "We'd welcome the company," replied the
Georgian. He extended his hand, even though the muscles
of his arm burned like pure fire. "My name's John Slocum
and this here's Sean O'Brady."

The old man traded handshakes, then parked himself
between the two men. "Pleased to meet you both. My

name's Gus Ferguson." He eyed the man to his right. "I'd say that you hail from the South, don't you?"

"That's right," said Slocum. "Georgia."

"I was born and bred in Alabama myself," Gus told him. "But, hell, that was well over sixty-odd years ago. I'm seventy-nine now, and since my thirteenth birthday, I've made just about everywhere my home but Alabam. In fact, I was fighting Injuns and risking my darn fool neck before Ol' Horace Greeley even told you young whippersnappers to 'go west.' Yep, I've seen my share of history in the making. The James and Youngers' downfall at Northfield, the meeting of the Union and Southern Pacific railroads, the ruckus at Sutter's Mill back in '48 . . . I was there for them all."

"Sounds as if you were there since the beginning," said O'Brady, his blue eyes gleaming with interest. "But how did you end up in Alaska? And, most of all, imprisoned here in the Glory Hole?"

"First things first," said Gus. "During all my years of roaming from one territory to another, I've only had one weakness, besides whiskey and woman, that is. And that weakness is gold. I hear a rumor of gold being discovered, and the fever hits me quicker than a whore's wink. I've mined and panned my share of claims in California, Colorado, and the Comstock in Nevada. Never found enough nuggets to make me rich, just enough to squander on liquor and crooked poker games. Then came word of the gold found here in the Alaska territory. Well, I took the first steamer up here, determined to finally make my fortune."

Satisfied that he held the two men's attention, Gus Ferguson continued. "I've been up here three years now, which makes me a true-blue sourdough. I've panned for gold near Nome, hiked the Suslota Pass from Valdez to Fairbanks, and spent the winter in the Chilkoot near the port of Skagway. But in all that time, I scarcely found enough gold to fill what little teeth I have left in my head. Then, last spring, I was drinking in a saloon in Eagle City when I heard tell of a gold strike somewhere in the mountains northwest of Nulato. I joined up with a group of fellow miners, and together, we headed up here to find it. Well, we were fifty miles north of the Kanuti River when we were ambushed in a mountain pass. A dozen men with rifles and scatterguns got the drop on us, then put us in chains. That big Eskimo Kolabuk was one of them. They marched us across the mountains for eight days, until we ended up here. They herded us into this mine at gunpoint, and I haven't seen the light of day since."

"And how long ago has that been?" asked Slocum.

"It's hard to tell," admitted Gus Ferguson. "I reckon seven or eight months ago. Been a helluva stay, I'll sure tell you that. Just one day of backbreaking work after another. I nearly died of pneumonia three months ago, but I fought it off. Told myself that I'd be damned if I was gonna die in this hole in the mountainside. If I do go to meet my maker, I want it to be outside in the sunshine, not in the darkness beneath tons of solid rock."

Slocum and O'Brady looked at each other. They couldn't help but admire the fiery old prospector.

"Exactly what do you know about the Glory Hole?" asked O'Brady.

"Not much. I do know that it's owned by some bastard named King and that he was the one who made up the story about a gold strike, just to lure men to the mountains so they could be caught and used as slaves. And, from what I've gathered, the Glory Hole has only been in operation a couple of years at most. Also, I've overheard talk that the claim ain't rightly King's. Seems that he cheated some trusting soul and took it for his own. It'd have to be a sorry son of a bitch who'd do a thing like that."

"We've met the man," said Slocum. "And, take it from us, he's even worse than you think."

Gus thought to himself for a moment. "Did you happen to come across a pretty Eskimo girl named Selana by any chance?" he asked.

Slocum saw red. "She was the one who sprung the trap on me."

"Well, to tell the truth, I'd say she was forced to do it. You see, Selana is Kolabuk's sister. The son of a bitch sold her to King for a bag of gold nuggets."

"What a Judas!" declared O'Brady.

Slocum felt his contempt toward the woman melt away. He couldn't rightly fault her for doing something that she more than likely had done out of fear for her life.

Their talk turned to other subjects. Gus Ferguson pointed out some of the more spirited of the Glory Hole's veterans. Then he nodded toward a short, skinny fellow who sat hunkered against a far wall, away from the others. "He's a right odd one," said Gus. "Name's Blake and he keeps mostly to himself. Works his share like the rest of us, but won't talk much. And another strange thing is that he won't take a shower at the falls with the rest of us. He always waits till after everyone's asleep, then goes to wash. A right sissified feller, like one of them dandies from back East. Can't even grow whiskers like a full-grown man. Don't know how he came to be here. Finch and some of the Eskimo guards tossed him in here a couple months ago. Said they found him wandering through the mountains for no good reason."

Slocum turned his attention to the man they were discussing. He was lean and slight of stature, and his clothing hung loosely upon his body. He wore a floppy hat over his head, and his face was long and thin, almost delicately so.

His hair was dark and cropped closely to his head.

As their talk covered other ground, Slocum decided it wouldn't hurt to mention the possibility of escape to the elderly prospector. Ferguson's ancient eyes glimmered with excitement. "If you get ready to take the chance, be sure to include me. I ain't nearly as feeble as I look to be. If I was, I wouldn't have lasted this long in the Hole. Besides, I know this territory like the back of my hand. I can guide you back to St. Michael with no trouble at all."

Slocum and O'Brady promised him that they would give it some thought. But, already they knew that Gus Ferguson would prove to be invaluable as far as their survival beyond the Glory Hole was concerned. If anyone could lead them safely back to the Alaskan seaport of St. Michael, it was the savvy old sourdough with the bushy gray beard.

Slocum looked at the old man, and a question suddenly came to mind. "Gus . . . exactly how many men came to the mountains with you, looking for that bogus gold strike?"

A haunted expression hung heavily in Ferguson's eyes. "There were nine of us in all."

"And how many of you are left?"

"Just myself," he said in reply. "The rest have already died, one way or the other."

Silence replaced any further conversation. As each man turned to his own thoughts, Slocum knew his worst suspicions had been confirmed by what little Gus had told them. More than ever, he felt the need to escape the chains of the Glory Hole, although it might seem impossible to do so.

13

January gradually drew on into February. Time meant little in the black dungeon of the Glory Hole, but Slocum was determined to keep track nevertheless. He kept count by placing a pebble in his trouser pocket each night before he fell asleep. It wasn't long before one pocket grew heavy with stones and he had to resort to using the other.

Their daily chores varied depending on which crew was assigned which task, but none seemed to be any easier than the other. Either they worked on the veins of gold that crisscrossed the cavern walls, loaded the precious metal into ore cars, or pushed the heavy carts through the tunnel to the elevator that would carry them to the uppermost level. Others worked the winch that operated the elevator or labored in the harsh sub-zero weather, emptying the cars into the wooden bins on the side of the mountain. No matter what job a prisoner labored at during a sixteen-hour shift, he always returned to the cavern on the seventh level dog-tired and broodingly quiet. Some were carried back by their fellow slaves, having passed out from exhaustion or creeping illness.

On the twentieth day of February, Slocum reviewed what had happened in the month that he had been imprisoned there. Three of the sixty-seven had died during that time— one of pneumonia, one due to a rock slide, and one because of gangrene that set in when he accidently pierced his foot with a misplaced swing of a pickax. No form of ceremony was provided for those who had perished. Kolabuk and his men simply wrapped the bodies up in canvas and hauled them through the connecting tunnel to the elevator. In his heart, Slocum was certain that the dead men had not been given a decent burial as they deserved. More than likely, their corpses had been dumped down the steep grade of the mountainside, to appease the hungry wolves that roamed the passes below in search of food.

Those who showed disrespect toward Gastineau or the others, or tried to stir up trouble of any sort, were treated the way that a disobedient animal might be. Sometimes Gastineau or Kolabuk would hand their guns to a guard and subject the troublemaker to a brutal beating. Both the Canadian and the Eskimo were big, brawny men who knew how to box and brawl, as well as use a dozen dirty tricks such as sucker punches and unexpected kicks to the groin. Usually they would beat the disgruntled prisoner within an inch of his life, then leave him bruised and bleeding on the cave floor.

Some were handled in a different manner. They were tied to the column of one of the cavern's stalagmites and given fifty lashes across the naked back with a bullwhip. Gastineau derived pleasure from the whippings he administered, but not nearly as much as Kolabuk did. The Eskimo relished the groans of pain and the scent of blood in the air. Sometimes he would stop halfway through a whipping and rub salt or spit raw tobacco juice into the open wounds, then continue the flogging, increasing the victim's torment tenfold. Many who suffered at the cruel hand of Kolabuk passed out from sheer agony before they received their fiftieth lash.

It was at times such as those that Slocum found himself watching Casey Elder. The Negro giant would stand among the other workers and silently watch the whippings. Outwardly, his face appeared emotionless, as if he didn't care one way or the other. But Slocum sensed what the black man felt just beneath the surface. He noticed the anger that burned in Elder's dark eyes and saw the way the man's shoulders flinched slightly with each crack of the bullwhip. The former slave obviously recalled the days when he himself had been subjected to such inhumane treatment, perhaps by the hand of a sadistic master or plantation overseer. But, somehow, Elder managed to keep his emotions in check. He never let his feelings show as he quietly watched the beatings, and then, afterward, he returned to his work, putting even more power behind the swing of his sledge than he had before.

Slocum knew that it was only a matter of time before Casey Elder could no longer contain his hatred toward Kolabuk and Henri Gastineau. Sooner or later, he was bound to lose control and strike out before he could stop himself. Elder was a proud man who had felt the sting of the bullwhip and the chafing of shackles on his ankles and wrists, and Slocum knew that his contempt only grew with each beating or whipping that his fellow captives were subjected to.

It happened during a shift near the end of February.

Slocum and several others had been assigned the task of pushing the loaded ore cars through the tunnel to the shaft that would carry them to the ground level. Gus Ferguson and Sean O'Brady pushed one car, while Slocum and Casey Elder pushed another. They had delivered perhaps a dozen loads when the incident took place. Slocum and Elder were about to haul another carload from the cavern, when Kolabuk decided that they weren't moving fast enough.

"Get moving!" growled the big Eskimo. "Do you understand me, you damned nigger? I said to move!"

It was at that moment that Casey Elder could no longer keep a rein on his true feelings. He stopped dead still in the center of the tracks, his dark hands gripping the edge of the ore cart until the knuckles bulged with strain. Then he said a single word. "No."

Kolabuk glared at the Negro, looking a little puzzled. "What did you say to me, nigger?"

The black man turned his massive head. Rage blazed in his eyes. "I said no, that's what I said. And my name ain't 'nigger.' It's Elder."

The big Eskimo stared at the Negro for a long moment, then laughed incredulously. "I don't give a damn what your name is. All I know is that you are going to move . . . right now." And with that, he took the coiled whip from his belt and unfurled it.

Elder waited until Kolabuk cocked his arm back and brought the length of braided leather whistling through the air, aiming the tip for the expanse of the Negro's broad back. Then, swiftly, he whirled on his heels. His massive hand shot out and grabbed hold of the end of the whip. With a powerful jerk, Elder wrenched the haft of the bullwhip completely from Kolabuk's grasp, then tossed the wicked instrument of torture over his shoulder, into the gloom of the cavern.

Kolabuk simply stood there, unable to believe what had happened. The other prisoners and the guards who watched over them reacted in the same startled way. Elder had never caused trouble before; in fact he had seemed to go out of his way to avoid it. But here he was facing down the brawny Eskimo with no sign of fear or regret in his eyes.

"You just made a bad mistake, nigger!" growled Kolabuk through gritted teeth. He reached around and took hold of the Sharps that was slung over his back. A second later, he had the iron hammer cocked and the muzzle leveled squarely at Elder's chest.

Some in the cave expected the Negro to realize his error and drop to his knees, pleading for mercy. But Slocum knew the black man better than that. He reacted exactly the way Slocum expected him to.

Casey Elder threw back his head and laughed. His voice rolled throughout the belly of the Glory Hole like rumbling thunder. "You turned out to be the coward I figured you to be, Kolabuk. If you were a true man, you'd put aside that rifle and fight me with your bare hands. But I reckon you're too yellow to do an honorable thing like that."

Kolabuk took Elder's bait without hesitation. With an angry roar, the Eskimo unslung his rifle, bow, and quiver, and tossed the bundle to a guard who stood nearby. "I'll teach you who is the man here!" he vowed, starting toward the huge Negro, his fists clenched and held at chest level. "When I get through with you, you'll beg me to end your miserable life!"

Elder merely laughed, even bolder than before. That sent Kolabuk into a frenzy. He rushed forward and swung powerfully at the black man's jaw. Elder refused to dodge the blow, however. He stood there and took the punch to the chin. His head rocked back, but only a little. Then he grinned and delivered his own blow. He caught Kolabuk in a haymaker that sent the big Eskimo spinning backward, his eyes dazed.

Kolabuk caught his balance before he could hit the ground. He steadied himself and lifted his hand to his left cheekbone. Elder's knuckles had split the skin, and blood coated the Eskimo's palm. Kolabuk's fury calmed a bit, turning quickly into caution. He brought up his fists again and motioned for the Negro to approach him. Elder did just that, lifting his own ham-size fists and walking in slow.

The two squared off and sized each other up. The prisoners and guards who gathered in a circle around them sized them up also, but no one could tell who had the advantage. Casey Elder had the height and weight over Kolabuk, but the Eskimo was faster and meaner. Everyone was anxious to see who would end up the victor in the contest of brute force.

A moment later, the two men closed the gap between them. Fists lashed out furiously, bruising flesh and bringing blood. Kolabuk delivered a flurry of solid punches to Elder's head, breaking his nose and battering his left eye until it swelled shut. The Negro, in turn, assaulted Kolabuk from a different angle. He swung low, delivering mighty blows to the Eskimo's torso. Kolabuk groaned as one blow found the right side of his rib cage. There was a brittle crack as one of his ribs snapped cleanly in half.

Kolabuk staggered back and scowled at the sharp pain that shot threw his side. Then he bellowed a hoarse yell and started back toward the big Negro, more sluggishly than before. Elder dodged a roundhouse punch and again drove his fist low. This time his knuckles slammed squarely into Kolabuk's stomach. The Eskimo gagged and dropped to his knees, although he fought to stay on his feet.

Casey Elder had the man exactly where he wanted him. He looked over at his companions. No one uttered a single word, but their eyes cheered him on, urging him to finish the brawl. Slocum glanced over at the two guards who stood nearby. Their eyes were stunned and trained on their fallen boss, not on the captives who normally held their attention. Slocum then turned to O'Brady. The Irishman nodded, letting the Southerner know that he was aware of the chance that had presented itself. He began to move slowly toward one of the guards, while Slocum made his way inconspicuously toward the other.

But before they were able to overpower the two, the fight took a nasty turn. Elder grabbed a fistful of Kolabuk's long black hair and reared back with his right leg back, ready to smash his knee into the Eskimo's face. But Kolabuk wasn't about to be defeated, even if it meant fighting dirty. In desperation, he drew his bone-handled Bowie knife from the sheath on his belt and lashed out. Elder spotted the glint of steel out of the corner of his eye. He stepped back a few paces, but not nearly enough to escape the blade entirely. The Bowie's honed edge sliced through the material of Elder's shirt and cut deeply into the flesh underneath. Elder gasped as the blade sliced a groove from hipbone to belly button. The Negro clamped a hand to the wound, keeping his guts from spilling out and trying to stem the flow of blood.

Kolabuk stood up, ignoring the pain in his belly and ribs. With a cruel grin, he tightened his grip on the Bowie and took a step toward his injured foe. He would have surely used the knife on the Negro again, if Gastineau hadn't shown up at that moment.

"Leave him be, Kolabuk," ordered Gastineau. "You've damaged him enough."

Kolabuk looked at the Canadian as if he were crazy. "But why? Let me kill the black bastard, Gastineau."

"No!" said Gastineau flatly. "No matter what happened between the two of you, he's still the best worker we have in the Hole. He can do three times the work of any of these men standing here. If you kill him, the production we've built up in the past month will fall back down again. And Mr. King wouldn't like that one bit."

Kolabuk glared at Gastineau, then turned his angry eyes back to Casey Elder. He looked as though he were on the verge of disobeying Gastineau's orders, when he abruptly slid the Bowie back into its sheath and staggered away, cursing in his native tongue. Obviously, the threat of Arthur King's wrath was enough to hold him at bay. He knew that if he went against Gastineau, it would be considered an act of treason against their employer. And, in turn, he would likely be shot right there on the spot.

Henri Gastineau marched to where Casey Elder slumped against a boulder. He pulled the black man's hand away and frowned at the ugly wound in his abdomen. Then he turned to Gus Ferguson. "Can you doctor this man?" he asked the elderly prospector.

Gus nodded in agreement. "Bring me a needle and thread, clean bandages, and a bottle of hoochinoo, and I'll fix him up. He'll have to rest for a few days, though, to allow the wound to heal properly."

"All right," said Gastineau. He ordered one of the guards to fetch the things Gus would need from the bunkhouse above. "But just make sure that he lives. Remember, Elder is worth three of you. If you allow him to die, three of you will make up for his quota."

Gus glared at the Canadian. "He'll live. I've sewed up my share of knife wounds and bullet holes in my time."

A half hour later, Gus had the supplies he needed. It took six men to carry Casey Elder to the far side of the cave. They laid him under the light of a seal-oil lamp, then the old man went to work. First he doused the wound with the homemade liquor, drawing only a grunt from the proud black man. After the wound had been sterilized, Gus threaded the needle and slowly sewed the gash shut. It took seventy stitches to close the skin, but after an hour, the operation was completed. Gus poured hoochinoo over the wound again, but Elder said nothing this time. He had drunk his fill of the liquor while Gus stitched him up, and it had deadened his pain considerably.

After the bearded prospector finished, he expelled a sigh

of relief and took a long swallow of the hooch himself. "So why did you do such a stupid thing, Elder? You could've ended up with your innards hanging down around your feet."

Casey Elder shrugged his broad shoulders and grinned. "I don't know. I reckon I just had my fill of that slant-eyed bastard. Sure felt good putting him in his place for once, even if I did get stabbed doing it."

Gus Ferguson couldn't help but smile himself. "You sure gave him a whupping he won't soon forget, that's for sure." He turned to Slocum and O'Brady, who crouched nearby. "We almost had a chance, didn't we?"

Slocum nodded. "We came close, but we missed it when Kolabuk pulled that Bowie. But don't worry. It'll come again."

"Yeah," said Gus grimly. "Maybe one of these days."

The Negro reached out and clasped Gus's spidery hand. "Whatever you fellows are talking about, count me in the next time that chance comes. I'll do anything in my power to help you. I owe you that much for sewing my belly up."

"I might just hold you to that promise, Elder," said the old man, patting the black man on the shoulder. "But you won't be doing much of anything for a while. Now, just lay back and rest."

Elder didn't have to be told twice. A moment later, the hooch had taken effect, lulling him into a deep sleep.

Slocum thought about the chance for escape that had slipped through their fingers. It left a bitter taste in his mouth, but he didn't despair. As Gus said, they would come across another someday. Slocum just hoped that it would present itself soon, while they were still physically able to take advantage of the opportunity.

14

The month of February was coming to a close when a tragic incident occurred in the Glory Hole, an incident that presented a startling discovery—as well as something of a dilemma—for John Slocum.

It took place shortly after the midday meal. The cavern of gold-veined walls was full of activity. Crews of men wielded picks and sledgehammers, while others loaded the carts full of the newly mined gold. Once again, Slocum had been assigned to the crew that pushed the ore cars through the tunnel to the main shaft. Sean O'Brady and a longshoreman named Quincy pushed the cart ahead, while Slocum and the slight fellow named Blake struggled with their own. Behind them, Gus Ferguson and Casey Elder labored behind the weight of another car. The big Negro hadn't been out commission very long following his brawl with Kolabuk. Scarcely a week had passed before he was forced back to work.

They were delivering their third load of the day to the freight elevator, when Slocum heard something. It was a faint noise, like the rumbling of a distant thunderstorm. "Did you hear that?" he asked the man next to him.

The skinny fellow with the slouch hat and dirty but beardless face simply shook his head. Slocum had attempted to strike up a conversation several times with the man, but he had declined every effort the Southerner had made. Slocum

107

had finally decided that it wasn't worth the trouble. Some men just weren't as sociable as others.

He was about to turn and ask Gus if he had heard the distant rumble, when it came again, this time much louder and closer than before. Dust trickled from the ceiling overhead, and Slocum saw the walls of the tunnel shift slightly. Then came the unnerving crack of a support beam splintering. Slocum looked back at the front of the tunnel just in time to see a sturdy length of timber break in half and bow inward. He also saw who was standing beneath the support at that particular moment.

"Sean!" he yelled out, but there was no point in even trying to warn the Irishman. One end of the beam swung downward and struck O'Brady in the side of the head. The force was such that the Irishman's skull swung unnaturally to the side, to rest on the slope of his shoulder. Slocum could tell in an instant that his friend's neck had been fatally broken by the falling timber.

Then, a second later, ton upon ton of loose rock and earth dropped downward like a murderous curtain, crushing O'Brady and the men ahead of him beneath a hail of solid stone. A wave of dust rolled through the tunnel, and suddenly, Slocum found himself being swept backward by the impact of the avalanche. He tumbled head over heels, spinning past the ore car behind him and landing next to Gus, who had also been knocked off his feet by the force of the cave-in. Ahead of him, Slocum could hear Blake cry out in alarm. His voice came out high and shrill, far from masculine. The Georgian sensed more surprise than hurt in that cry and knew that his partner for that day had not been severely injured.

Almost as swiftly as it had begun, the avalanche of stone and earth settled. The rumbling overhead stopped, and they knew that it was safe to move once again. Slocum climbed to his feet and steadied himself with the aid of an ore cart. He peered ahead of him, but he could see nothing. The impact of the cave-in had extinguished the seal-oil lamps that hung along the tunnel walls, and a heavy pall of dust hung in the air.

"O'Brady!" he called out, though not loud enough to cause any more tremors. "Can you hear me, Sean?"

Slocum felt a spidery hand rest on his muscular shoulder. "Of course he can't," came the grim voice of Gus Ferguson. "You saw that support beam hit him the same as I did. O'Brady's dead, there's no two ways about it."

The tall Southerner swallowed dryly and knew that Gus was right. Even if the Irishman had not been killed by the falling timber, there was absolutely no way he could have survived the tons of rock and earth that had buried him and the other gold miners.

"Let's check it out," suggested the deep voice of Casey Elder. Together, the three stepped over mounds of earth and refuse, making their way to the blocked end of the tunnel.

What they found there was not at all encouraging. A sloping mound of huge boulders sealed off the tunnel from ceiling to floor. Elder attempted to move a couple of the stones away, but they were much too heavy for even him to handle. After pushing only a couple aside, the Negro's breathing grew labored and he was forced to stop.

Gus pressed an ear to the side of a flat boulder and listened as he rapped on it with bony knuckles. "Must be eight or nine feet of solid rock between us and the far side of the tunnel, maybe more."

"Do you hear anything?" asked Elder.

"Not yet," replied the old prospector. "But I trust Gastineau and his men will be digging us out soon. They'd likely leave us in here to rot, but it's the only way into the heart of the Glory Hole. Still, it'll be several hours yet."

Slocum suddenly remembered his partner on the ore car. "Blake? Where are you?"

A moment later, he heard a ragged coughing from the swirling cloud of dust that hung within the tunnel. Blindly, Slocum felt his way along the cluttered tracks until he reached the man. From the way Blake hacked and strangled, Slocum knew that he had inhaled a lot of loose dust and was having trouble breathing. He knew he had to get Blake to the cavern, where the air was clearer and more plentiful.

It was when Slocum crouched behind Blake and encircled his chest with his arms, preparing to drag him bodily from the tunnel, that the Georgian made his discovery. Beneath the folds of Blake's shirt and coat, he felt something round and cushiony . . . or rather *two* things. It took Slocum a moment before he realized exactly what he was feeling.

Breasts. Blake had breasts—small, but perfectly formed.

Confused, Slocum paused and, in the darkness, explored further. He ran a hand over Blake's cheeks and chin. Oddly enough, the skin was as smooth as silk and utterly devoid of whiskers. Then he grew bolder and felt along the front of Blake's baggy trousers. Just as he suspected, there was nothing there. No manhood bulged at the crotch; only the fleshy crease common to the female gender.

Well, I'll be damned! thought Slocum. Blake is a woman!

He decided to ponder the questions in his head later. In the meantime, he tightened his hold around Blake's waist and dragged him—or rather *her*—away from the thick mist of earth that hung heavily in the tunnel. Soon, the two were back in the main cavern of the Glory Hole. Slocum leaned Blake's body against a wall. The worker's coughing decreased as dust was rapidly replaced with deep breaths of pure air.

"Are you all right?" asked Slocum.

As he stared into Blake's eyes, he saw something there that he had not noticed there before, even during months of laboring side by side together. He detected an expression of tenderness there, as well as gratitude. Blake said nothing in reply, just nodded and uttered one last lung-clearing cough.

"Just like I thought," said Gus Ferguson as he and Casey Elder emerged from the tunnel, shaking dust and rock from their arms and legs. "I took another listen to that boulder, and I could hear the sound of hammers and picks already. It'll be a couple of hours, but that confounded Canadian and his men oughta break through eventually."

Slocum glanced at the seated form of Blake, then looked back at Gus and Casey. Suddenly, he was forced to make a decision. Should he tell them about his discovery? He only had to look around him to find the answer. Perhaps forty or fifty men stood within earshot. All were hard-edged and desperate men, weary of their imprisonment and the degrading way that Gastineau and Kolabuk had treated them; men who ached for some way to release their anger and frustration. They were also men who had not enjoyed the company of a woman for a very long time. Slocum could picture what might possibly take place if Blake's secret were revealed, and it was not a very pretty picture to look at.

So, being the Southerner that he was, John Slocum decided to do the honorable thing. He kept his mouth shut.

The three guards who had watched over the workers in the Glory Hole that day lost no time. They herded the laborers into one group and surrounded them, keeping their rifles cocked and aimed at all times. Slocum could tell by their eyes that they were scared shitless and expected the prisoners to rush them at any moment. Slocum turned that possibility over in his mind, but abandoned it after a little thought. All three guards held repeating rifles—two sported lever-action Winchesters and one an old Spencer carbine—and they would likely pick off seven or eight men before they themselves were overtaken. And, from the way the prisoners refrained from making any threatening moves, Slocum knew that no one was stupid enough to make the first move and put his life on the line for the sake of his fellow captives.

So they simply sat there on the floor of the cavern, waiting for their rescuers to make their appearance. It came three hours later. They heard the sound of rolling stones echo from the mouth of the tunnel, followed by the sound of voices. Then came the crisp pace of footsteps. They turned their eyes toward the tunnel, relieved that the only route to leave the Glory Hole had been successfully unblocked.

The first to appear from the tunnel was Henri Gastineau, followed by Kolabuk. They, too, seemed relieved, but not because the majority of the work force had survived the cave-in. Rather, they seemed glad that the main chamber of the Glory had not suffered from the avalanche. Obviously, they had the best interest of their employer foremost in their minds.

"O'Brady?" Gus asked as Gastineau drew near. "Did you find him back in there?"

"We found the bodies of several men as we broke through," said the French-Canadian without concern. "Or, rather, what was left of them. Tons of solid rock can make a godawful mess of a man's body, you know."

Gastineau's disregard for the lives of his workers angered Slocum to no end. He had to grit his teeth and lock his muscles to keep from launching himself at the burly man.

After taking a head count, Gastineau sighed deeply. "Dammit! It looks like I figured correctly. We lost ten men to that blasted cave-in!" He then turned his eyes to those who had survived. "Well, I suppose that means only one thing. All of you will have to make up for the loss of your fellow miners. Now, get up and get back to work! You'll finish this shift as usual, and you will not stop until today's quota is filled."

No one in the cave could believe the Canadian's nerve. There they had been trapped in a cave-in that had taken the lives of ten of their fellow workers, and all that the foreman worried about was failing to fulfill the daily goal set by Arthur King.

The eyes of every prisoner in the dark belly of the Glory Hole were filled with hatred for the man named Henri Gastineau. If sheer emotion could kill, the Canadian would have died several dozen times. But, unfortunately, their contempt, in itself, held no power. Gastineau simply laughed and instructed his guards to keep a watchful eye on the slaves and make sure that they did as they were told.

Eventually, they were forced to do just that, knowing that rebellion at that moment would only bring death and agonizing injury. As he picked up a pickax and began to tackle one of the veins in the cavern wall, Slocum glanced over at the one who labored next to him. Blake hefted a sledgehammer in lean but work-hardened fists and awkwardly began to pound away at the wall. Just one look at the laborer's eyes told Slocum that no one hated Gastineau or his men nearly as much as she did. There seemed to be some personal edge to her contempt, as if she possessed some reason for despising them other than the obvious ones.

And, as Slocum went to work himself, he told himself that he would find out what that reason was . . . when the right time presented itself.

15

Later that night, Slocum found his chance to explore the mystery of Blake further and find out exactly why she had been confined to the Glory Hole with the rest of the enslaved gold miners.

A couple of hours had passed since that day's grueling shift ended, and the prisoners were fast asleep. Only Slocum was awake. He was exhausted from the pace they had been subjected to following the cave-in, but he was more interested in discovering the truth about Blake than in catching a few hours' sleep before the morning call roused them back to work.

Quietly, Slocum rose from his blankets and made his way through the gloom of the cavern, trying to pick Blake from the others who lay along the sloping wall. Most of the seal-oil lamps had been extinguished, and there were no guards present in the underground chamber. Since the tunnel leading to the main shaft was the only access the prisoners had to the outside world, only one guard was posted, at the far end of the tunnel, from ten o'clock to five o'clock the following morning. The guard on duty was always well armed, cradling a sawed-off twelve-gauge in his lap. If one or more captives had even attempted to make it to the mouth of the shaft, the guard would have unleashed a blast of double-aught buckshot, wiping out the bunch before they could get within twenty feet.

As carefully as possible, Slocum stepped over the sleeping bodies, searching for the right one. He spotted Blake curled up near a stalagmite close to the waterfall, several yards away from the others. Silently, he knelt next to the sleeping form and studied Blake's face in the faint glow of a nearby lantern. Despite the dirt and the shortness of her dark brown hair, the woman appeared almost angelic in the flickering light. Studying the lean beauty of her face, as well as her doe-like eyes and the fullness of her lips, Slocum knew it was a miracle that no one had seen through her disguise before now. But then, when a man was sentenced to an existence of hard labor and despair in a place such as the Glory Hole, he was more apt to concentrate on his own misery and not pay much attention to those who suffered around him.

Slocum reached out and laid a hand on Blake's shoulder. Almost instantly, the woman came awake. She recoiled slightly at the sight of Slocum looming over her, her eyes startled. Slocum sensed a cry rising in her throat and clamped his hand over her mouth, keeping the scream from escaping. "I'm not going to hurt you," he whispered softly. "I just want to talk to you."

When he took his hand away, Blake tried to appear more angry than frightened. "What the hell do you want?" she asked in a gruff but subdued voice.

"There's no need to keep up your act with me," assured Slocum. "I know what you are. I just want to know how you came to be here." When the fearful expression in her eyes failed to diminish, Slocum spoke again. "Really, I promise I'm not going to harm you in any way. And I'm not about to expose you to the others. That would be like throwing a lamb to a pack of wolves in a hellhole like this."

The woman calmed a little, sensing the sincerity in Slocum's eyes. "Let's go somewhere where we can talk without being overheard," she suggested, her voice gentle and utterly devoid of the masculine tone she had used in the past.

Together, they left the scattering of sleeping men and made their way toward the waterfall. They stopped at a deep crevice in the cavern wall and ducked into the shadows. The roar of the underground spring was loud enough that it masked their voices, enabling them to talk freely without being overheard.

"All right, let's start from the beginning," said Slocum. "Who are you and what are you doing here of all places?"

The woman hesitated at first, then decided it would do no harm to confide in the tall Southerner. "My name is Blake Duboise," she began. "I am an actress of the theater, Shakesphere mostly. I've toured all over the country— New York, Boston, St. Louis, San Francisco . . . I've even performed for the crowned heads of Europe. As for how I came to be here, it is really due to my father, Charles Duboise. He, too, is an actor, but he sometimes abandons his profession to engage in his second love. That is fortune-hunting. Since he was a young man, my father has traveled the world in search of riches. He will vanish for a year or two, embark on some wild goose chase, then reappear with scarcely a cent in his pocket.

"His latest disappearance, however, seemed to have netted him the fortune he has always sought," she continued. "Three years ago, he bid my family and me farewell and set off for the Alaskan territory in search of gold. We expected Father to encounter the same disappointment that he always did, but quite the contrary occurred. A year after his disappearance, I received a package from him. It contained a long letter, proclaiming that he had discovered a mother lode in the northern mountains. Also in the package was a chunk of gold the size of a man's fist and a crude map showing the location of Father's claim. Needless to say, the Duboise family was overjoyed. But, unfortunately, our excitement was short-lived."

"What happened?" asked Slocum, although he could imagine where her story was leading.

"Several months after I received Father's package, another letter came. This time he expressed concern over something that had happened immediately after his discovery of the gold mine. It appeared that a powerful man named Arthur King caught wind of the enormity of his claim and had made several attempts to purchase it from him. Father's refusal to part with his 'Glory Hole,' as he called it, only seemed to anger King. Father was severely beaten once and almost killed by a sniper's bullet a second time. His letter expressed his fear, and he asked me to contact my brother in San Francisco, in hopes of recruiting some help in order to stop the dishonest miser."

"Your brother?" asked Slocum.

"Yes," replied Blake. "Andrew Duboise."

Slocum had heard the name before. "The Pinkerton agent?"

"The very same. Anyway, I took a train from Denver to San Francisco and showed my brother Father's most recent letter. He read a menace between the lines that had at first escaped me. He was so concerned that he booked the first steamer for Alaska. Despite his protests, I insisted on accompanying him. He tried to discourage me, saying that such a harsh land was no place for a woman, but he failed in his efforts. Anyone who knows me well knows that once I set my mind to a task, I rarely change my mind."

Slocum smiled to himself in the darkness. He had only known the lady named Blake Duboise a short time, and already, he couldn't help but admire her spirit. Obviously, it was that strength that had allowed her to survive in the dark pit of the Glory Hole.

"A month later, Andrew and I arrived at the port of St. Michael," she continued. "We asked around town, hoping to locate our father, but no one seemed even to know who he was. My impression was that no one wanted to talk to us, mostly out of fear. I knew immediately that the scoundrel Arthur King was behind it all. I wanted to confront him, face-to-face, but Andrew assured me that such an action would do more harm than good. Instead, he suggested that we travel to the mountains and search for Father's claim. We had the map giving its exact location, so it seemed like the best thing to do. It was the height of summer, so we took a flatboat up the Yukon. Before we left St. Michael, however, both of us decided that it would be best if I wore a disguise. I'd heard that there were fifty men for every one woman in Alaska, and I thought it would prevent trouble during our journey if I were to keep my gender a secret. I cut my hair short and dressed in men's clothing. My theatrical training enabled me to change my mannerisms and deepen my voice. All in all, I proved to be a very convincing gentlemen."

"You sure fooled everyone here," Slocum told her.

In the gloom, Slocum could barely see the woman smile. It was a lovely smile, one that tugged at the Georgian's heart, as well as his libido.

"We hoped to reach the mountains before bad weather overtook us, but, unfortunately, the seasons here are not like they are back home. There is no autumn even to speak of. Winter hit suddenly and without warning. We were a week from the settlement of Nulato when a treacherous blizzard engulfed us. Andrew tried his best to follow the route shown on Father's map, but it was difficult. One mountain pass looked like a dozen others. Soon, we became helplessly lost. For days, we wandered through the mountains, unable to find the pass that lead to Father's Glory Hole. Our supplies began to dwindle, and eventually, the horses we had bought in Nulato could no longer travel through the deepening snowdrifts. As the temperature dropped, first one animal froze to death and then the other. After that, we were forced to travel every step of the way by foot."

Blake Duboise paused for a moment, and Slocum could hear her breathing deepen, as if she recalled something that she wished she could forget. When she continued with her story, there was a painful edge to her voice. "Three weeks after we first entered the mountains, my brother fell victim to this godforsaken land. The night before, we had set up camp beneath the ledge of a cliff, in order to seek shelter from the wind. The next morning I awoke and turned to where Andrew had fallen asleep. In his place was a huge mound of snow. A drift had fallen from the lip of the cliff in the dead of night and completely buried him. Why I hadn't heard it fall, I have no earthly idea. Perhaps I was so exhausted that nothing could have roused me. In any case, I rushed to the mound and, with my bare hands, dug down until I found my brother. Andrew was dead. The snow had smothered him and he was frozen solid. I almost gave up then, but I knew it was up to me to find the gold mine, and Father, if he were still alive. I buried Andrew in the drift once again, said a prayer over his grave, then pressed onward."

"But you eventually found the Glory Hole," said Slocum.

"Yes, but rather unexpectedly. I stumbled upon the mining camp, thinking that I had finally made it to my destination. Instead, it proved to be my worst nightmare. Gastineau and his men captured me, shackled my ankles, and brought me down here to work in the gold mine. It took all I had to endure the work I was forced to do, but I vowed that I would do my share. I knew that if I didn't, Gastineau and Kolabuk would find out my secret—and then I would suffer a fate much worse than the Glory Hole."

Slocum knew that she was right. More than likely, Blake would have been brutally raped by Gastineau and his men, then subjected to a degrading existence as their bunkhouse whore, forced to provide pleasure on command. If anything would have broken the spirit of the brave woman who stood next to him, it would have been a fate such as that.

"I told everyone that my surname was Blake, thinking that Gastineau might grow suspicious if I used the name Duboise," said the woman. "I've tried my best to keep my secret from the others, and I've been successful . . . until now."

"Like I said before, your secret is safe with me," Slocum assured her. "But what about your father?"

Again, emotional agony sounded in Blake's voice. "I overheard Gastineau and Kolabuk talking one day. From what they said, it appeared that Father was killed by King's men and the deed to his claim stolen. And, from the way I heard it, my father wasn't the only one. Others have suffered a similar fate after they refused King's offers to buy their claims. That, in itself, shows what a cold-blooded bastard the man is."

"Amen to that," said Slocum in total agreement.

Quietly, Slocum told the woman of his plans to escape the Glory Hole whenever the chance presented itself. He assured her that when the time came to leave the hellish gold mine, she would go with him. Then he thought of something. "The map your father sent you? Where is it?"

A sly gleam shone in Blake's eyes. "It's sewn into the lining of my coat. Gastineau and his men took everything else from me before they brought me down here. The map is the only thing I have left to remember my father by. Some days, it is the only thing that keeps me going."

"It could come in handy during our escape, too," Slocum explained. "Old Gus claims that he can get us back to St. Michael with his eyes closed, but if he's wrong, the map could help get us there."

Blake patted the folds of her ragged coat. "It's here if you need it."

For a moment, both stood there in the gloom of the crevice, saying nothing. Slocum could sense the woman's body close by, and he ached to reach out for her, but he refrained from doing so. He heard Blake's breath quicken and knew that, she, too, felt the same attraction.

"Thank you for keeping my secret, Slocum," she said, her face scarcely a foot away from his.

"John," he corrected.

"John then," she said, and once again, he saw the paleness of her feminine smile blaze through the darkness. "I suppose we should get some rest now. We have a hard day's work ahead of us come morning."

"Yes," replied Slocum with a sigh of resignation. "But this hell won't last forever. I promise you that."

"I hope you are right," said Blake. The woman's hand clasped his for a long moment, then she left the crevice and returned to her rightful place beside the cavern wall.

Slocum stood there in the darkness for a while, fighting off the desire that threatened to possess him. The tall Southerner was a passionate man who had had his share of women in the past. And Blake Duboise was just the kind of woman that appealed to his manly instincts the most.

16

Several days had passed since Slocum learned the true nature of Blake Duboise and the reason for her imprisonment in the Glory Hole. As time passed, the tall Georgian had come to admire—and desire—the enslaved actress even more than he had following their secret conversation in the crevice of the cavern wall.

During the day's long work shift, Slocum found his thoughts divided between the regiment of backbreaking work, his private plans for escape, and, of course, Blake Duboise. Every now and then, he would turn and regard the woman as she labored, side by side, with the unsuspecting miners around her. From the way she wielded a hammer or pick, and carried her share of the load despite the slightness of her height and weight, Slocum figured that pioneer blood had run in her family sometime in the past. Blake possessed the spirit and tenacity of those rugged women who had bravely accompanied their men into the wilderness of the unsettled West and fought Indians and the harshest conditions that nature could conjure.

Strangely enough, Slocum didn't seem to be the only one who was paying closer attention to Blake lately. The Southerner had caught Gastineau eyeing her several times when he swaggered through the Glory Hole, inspecting the pace of the crews and the quotas they were forced to fill. From the way the Canadian studied Blake, Slocum couldn't tell whether the man had seen through her disguise or not. All he knew was that Gastineau seemed to hold some suspicion for Blake, although it was the elusive kind that the burly foreman couldn't quite put his finger on.

Existence in the belly of the gold mine failed to grow any easier. In fact, the deaths of the ten workers had made life much harder for them all. The loss had threatened to slow down the Glory Hole's production, but Gastineau and Kolabuk had made certain that such a setback wouldn't take place. They drove the crews hard, cutting meals to two a day instead of three and increasing the work pace to compensate for the ten pairs of strong arms that were now missing.

In turn, men who had once been passive with despair and hopelessness were gradually growing restless, pushed to the limits of physical and mental endurance by their captors. Slocum sensed the change of mood and knew that it was a potentially dangerous one. If an opportunity for escape was presented anytime soon, it would not be taken calmly and rationally. More than likely, such a chance would cause a full-scale riot. Tensions were so high that there was a strong possibility that Gastineau and his men would not be the only victims of the mutiny. Slocum could picture dozens of desperate men scrambling to be the first to escape the underground hell, and in the process, some of their fellow prisoners would end up dying because of it. That was not how Slocum, Gus Ferguson, and Casey Elder had planned their escape. Theirs had been a subtle and secretive one which would, in the long run, give them an edge for survival once they reached the frozen wilderness beyond the mine. If any of the others were involved, however, they could expect only chaos instead of triumph.

• • •

It was after a particularly torturous day in the gold mine that Slocum found himself lying awake in his blankets, unable to fall asleep. Normally, he had no trouble resting at all, most of his strength sapped by the strain of the sixteen-hour shift. But tonight, Slocum tossed and turned on the hard stone floor of the cavern, as if agitated by something he couldn't quite account for.

The Georgian lay there, enduring the noise of snoring around him and staring up at the fanglike stalagtites that hung from the cavern ceiling. Then, shortly after midnight, he caught a glimpse of stealthy motion out of the corner of his eye.

Quietly, he sat up and turned his head. In the soft glow of the oil lamps, Slocum saw the fleeting shadow of a human form as it made its way along the cavern wall, toward the cascading rush of the waterfall. He didn't have to look twice to recognize it as belonging to Blake Duboise.

Once again, the familiar pang of desire nagged at him, as it had since the night they had talked together. Slocum knew what she was up to and why she was being so secretive. He considered lying back down, figuring that he had no business spying on her. But another part of him yearned to see the woman in a different light—one not obscured by masculine clothing and a day's worth of dust and sweat.

As silently as possible, Slocum stood and, grasping the chain between his ankles so as not to cause any noise, made his way past the slumbering bodies of his fellow miners. When he neared the waterfall and knew that its roar would mask the clinking of the iron links, he let go of the chain and walked more freely.

Slocum clung to the shadows along the cavern wall and, slowly, inched his way around the back of the waterfall, which poured from a crevice in the ceiling overhead. From where he stood, Slocum could see the silhouette of Blake against the yellow glow of lamplight that shone from the far side of the cavern, while he himself remained unseen. Part of the Southerner felt a little ashamed about watching her, while another part of him felt no guilt whatsoever for the act of voyeurism.

Breathlessly, he watched as Blake stood near the edge of the pool. Scarcely six feet of open space stretched between the back of the waterfall and the damp wall of the cave. Satisfied that she was concealed from view, Blake first removed her slouch hat, then her coat, laying them both on a boulder nearby. Then, one button at a time, she began to unfasten the front of her baggy shirt. Slocum gasped quietly when the garment was peeled away and Blake's upper body was exposed, etched in soft light and clinging droplets of stray water. His hands had not lied to him before. The woman's breasts were small, barely a handful, but they were pert and perfectly formed. The nipples stood out starkly against the lamplight, as hard and rounded as the ends of revolver bullets.

Then, after Blake had cast her shirt aside, she began to work at the belt of her trousers. Soon, she had undone the buckle, and her oversized britches slipped from around her waist. There was no way that she could shed the pants completely. Due to the shackles, all of the miners were forced to shower with their britches pooled around their ankles. But Blake seemed more intent on enjoying a leisurely birdbath than a full shower.

Slocum felt the crotch of his own trousers tighten as he stood in the shadows and watched the near-naked woman begin to bathe. Blake took a bandanna from the pocket of her coat and, dipping the cloth in the warm spray of the falls, began to rub it slowly across her skin, starting at her face and neck, then slowly working her way downward to her breasts, arms, and back. The gritty filth of dirt and perspiration was scrubbed away, leaving only soft, clean skin. Slocum shifted his gaze to her lower body, relishing the sight of trim hips, tight buttocks, and long, shapely legs. The heat of lust coursed through the tall Southerner, filling his loins with an urge that was maddening.

Apparently, Blake Duboise was experiencing similar needs. Slocum watched as the bandanna washed hips, butt, and legs, then lingered at the dark thatch between her thighs. Blake worked the cloth in a slow, circular motion, rubbing it against the sensitive folds of her opening. Little by little, the pace of her rhythm increased, and Slocum saw her head arch backward and her mouth work noiselessly, opening and closing like a fish yearning for oxygen. Slocum expected her to succumb to the act of stimulation, but she seemed to have some difficulty in doing so.

In the back of his mind, Slocum knew that it wasn't his place to interrupt her nocturnal bath. But in the rage of passion that now overtook him, he really didn't give a damn. He stepped away from the shadowy wall and moved forward. "Blake," he said softly.

The woman tensed at the sound of his voice, her eyes frightened at first. Then she recognized him as he grew near. "John," she whispered, her voice urgent, almost pleading.

Slocum didn't hesitate any longer. He could see Blake's want for him burning in her soft brown eyes. A moment later, he was at the pool's edge. Blake stood there, trembling, for a long moment, then fell into Slocum's strong arms. They kissed as a fine mist of warm water engulfed them, their lips clutching hungrily. Unable to suppress the urge, Slocum snaked his tongue past her teeth, and she accepted it wantonly, greeting it with her own. Moans of longing emerged from the throats of man and woman, primal cries of passion demanding release.

Slocum's mouth pulled away, then began to descend, traveling along Blake's swanlike throat to the gentle swell of her breasts. As he sucked at the bud of a tit, Blake went to work as well. Her nimble fingers first undid the buttons of his chambray shirt, then the front of his trousers. Soon, Slocum felt the restriction of his clothing fall away. The warmth of the fall's spray covered his naked flesh, while the woman's hands caressed the bulging fullness of his work-hardened muscles.

He felt one of her hands slide searchingly down the flat washboard of his abdomen, finally taking hold of his manhood. He expected her to fondle and stroke him softly, but he was pleasantly surprised. Instead, she firmly grasped the object of her desire, kneading it like dough. Months of constant labor in the gold mine had strengthened the woman's hand, and it felt like a velvety vice around him.

"I've been thinking about this for days," she whispered huskily in his ear.

"So have I," he murmured. His lips moved against the areola of her left breast, sending delicious shivers down her spine.

"But how?" she asked, indicating the shackles that bound her ankles. "These damned chains—"

Slocum raised his head. His eyes blazed with raw passion. "I know how," he assured her. Then he rested his calloused hands upon her hips, turned her completely around, and laid her, belly down, across the curve of a boulder.

He moved in closer, running his hands along the firm muscles of her back to the flare of her buttocks. The flesh beneath his fingers was pebbled with goose bumps, even though the space behind the waterfall was uncommonly warm.

"What are you waiting for, John?" she moaned. "Give it to me! Now!"

Slocum delayed no longer. He leaned in and, with a thrust of his hips, entered her. He slid in easy; she was already wet and ready for him. For a moment, he simply stood there and relished the sensation of liquid warmth that engulfed him.

Blake purred like a cat, her hips beginning to buck impatiently. Slocum's urgency matched that of his partner. He began to feed it to her with bold, hard strokes. In response, Blake rocked back, then pulled away. Hips and buttocks slapped forcefully, increasing in pace.

The last time Slocum had been with a woman was well over two months ago, and that had been with the whore named Selana in San Francisco. Therefore, his control was considerably weakened by the urgency of his need. As their rutting quickened, Slocum felt his sap begin to rise, and he knew that he wouldn't last much longer. As it turned out, Blake was also unable to contain herself. Both man and woman shuddered violently as ecstasy gripped them. Slocum sensed a yell of pleasure building in Blake's throat, and he swiftly clamped his hand over her mouth, afraid that even the roar of the waterfall would not be loud enough to mute her cries.

Slowly, their mutual climax subsided. Exhausted, they collapsed limply across the boulder and lay there for a while. When they finally summoned the strength to rise, Slocum and Blake began to dress quietly. They said little to each other, the afterglow of their intimacy fading as they realized that they were still condemned to the same hell as before.

Slocum had buttoned his trousers and was about to slip on his shirt, when he suddenly sensed that someone was behind him. As he turned, a brawny form emerged from out of the shadows. A fist as hard as the iron head of a hammer smashed into his jaw, sending him falling to the edge of the pool.

Dazed, Slocum struggled to get up, fighting against the pain that throbbed through his lower face. As he rose, Slocum glanced up at his attacker. Oddly enough, he wasn't at all surprised to find Henri Gastineau standing before him, grinning wickedly from ear to ear.

17

"I'd stay down if I were you, Slocum," warned the big Canadian. He turned toward Blake with a leer. The woman hadn't finished dressing, and her upper body was still exposed. "This concerns only me and the lady."

Slocum's head cleared, and he finally got to his feet, if unsteadily so. He launched himself at Gastineau, but the burly foreman was ready for him. Gastineau sidestepped the Southerner's attack, delivering a powerful roundhouse punch. The Canadian's knuckles crashed into the side of Slocum's head, catching him across the left temple.

Pinpoints of light danced before Slocum's eyes, and he stumbled off balance. The Georgian was normally better with his fists than he was that night, but his strength and coordination had been severely weakened, both by that day's work and his stamina-draining encounter with Blake Duboise. Before he could recover from the blow, Gastineau followed up with a devastating kick to his stomach. Slocum doubled up and dropped to his knees, feeling as if everything, including his guts, were about to come rushing up.

Satisfied that Slocum would be out of the picture for a while, Gastineau turned back to the woman who cowered behind the waterfall. "So, my suspicions were right," he mused, flashing a predatory grin. "I felt that there was something strange about you from the beginning. Now I see what it was."

Self-consciously, Blake crossed her arms, attempting to conceal her bare breasts. "Stay away from me," she warned. "Stay away or, I swear, I'll scream!"

Gastineau merely laughed. "Then, by all means, scream until your heart's content," he invited. "But do you really think that your fellow workers will come to your rescue? Of course not. They'll hear the voice of a woman, and they will pounce on you like a pack of wild dogs after a bitch in heat. And you know as well as I do that they will not leave you alone until every last one of them has had his turn with you."

Blake shuddered at the thought. She knew that the Canadian was right. If she screamed, she would have much worse to deal with than Henri Gastineau. Fifty horny men would be there in a matter of seconds, driven by lust and fighting over her, perhaps destroying her in their mad rush for sexual release.

Gastineau moved toward her. When she attempted to avoid him, he reached out and grabbed her by the wrist, drawing her to him. Roughly, he grabbed one of her breasts. He squeezed it hard, savoring the expression of pain that crossed her lovely face. "You know, it would be a shame to keep you here in the mine, when you could prove much more useful elsewhere."

Blake could see the fire of lust building in the man's evil eyes. "Yes," he continued. "I believe I will make you my own private squaw. Then you could cook and clean and spread your legs whenever I commanded. How does that sound to you?"

"I would rather die in this confounded hellhole!" snapped Blake, her eyes flaring with defiance.

Gastineau laughed softly. "I'm afraid that the choice is not yours to make," he told her. A glint of cruelty shone in his smile. "But how do I know that you are even worth the trouble? I suppose I will have to find out now, before I take you up to the bunkhouse."

Abruptly, Gastineau pulled her closer, assaulting her mouth with his own. Coarse whiskers ripped at her lower face, and she gagged at the stench of his breath—an odious combination of hoochinoo, tobacco juice, and rotted particles of food. Then she felt his hand abandon her tit and creep its way downward. An instant later, it was unbuckling the front of her trousers, eager for what lay underneath.

The word "rape" screamed through Blake Duboise's mind. She fought wildly as Gastineau began to tug the britches down off her hips, but the man was much too strong to escape. Her heart leapt in her chest when she felt the bulge of his hardness pressing against her lower belly.

"Let go of her," a voice suddenly demanded from behind them. "Now!"

Gastineau's expression darkened. "You stupid—" he began, but before he could complete his sentence, it was cut short by a mouthful of fist. The Canadian rocked back on his heels, his hold on Blake loosening. As the woman scampered out of his reach, Gastineau spat a glob of blood and broken teeth onto the cavern floor. Enraged by his injury, he growled beneath his breath and started toward Slocum.

The Georgian had, fortunately, regained some of his bearings following the savage kick to his midsection. As Gastineau swung angrily at his head, Slocum ducked, delivering a flurry of blows to the Canadian's belly and rib cage. The punches seemed to take some of the wind out of Gastineau, but Slocum still refused to let up. He extended his leg and tripped the big man. Gastineau lost his balance and fell flat on his face next to the boulder.

Slocum delivered a sharp kick to the seat of the man's britches. "Get up, you son of a bitch," he taunted.

Slowly, Henri Gastineau rose to his feet. But when he turned around, he was no longer in the mood for fisticuffs. Instead, he held the Colt Navy in his right hand.

"Cowardly bastard," said Slocum as he stared down the muzzle of his own gun.

"I knew you wouldn't last the winter, Slocum," rasped Gastineau with a bloody and broken grin. "It is too bad. You were an excellent worker."

Slocum watched as Gastineau cocked the Colt's hammer and aimed the gun unerringly at the Southerner's head. As the Canadian's finger began to tense on the trigger, Slocum heard Blake utter a moan of fearful protest behind him.

Then, when it looked as though the end were imminent, something completely unexpected took place.

A hulking shadow emerged from the darkness of the cavern wall and loomed over Gastineau. The Canadian sensed that something was wrong, but too late. Abruptly, brawny black arms the thickness of railroad ties encircled Gastineau in a crushing bear hug. Startled, the foreman lost hold of the .36 revolver. It hit the stone floor of the cavern, but, luckily, it did not go off.

Henri Gastineau opened his mouth, as if to yell out for help, but the strong arms that imprisoned him tightened, allowing only a rattling gush of air to escape his lungs. His bearded face grew bright red, then began to darken, turning a deep shade of purple.

"Who?" asked Blake in wonder. But Slocum already knew who was responsible. Gradually, the attacker stepped into view. Casey Elder increased the pressure of his bear hug, an expression of supreme rage creasing his dark face. Behind him stood the skinny form of the old prospector Gus Ferguson.

Slocum and Blake watched as Gastineau's face developed a hue that was almost as black as that of his assailant's.

The sinews of Elder's arms flexed, and they could hear the muted cracking of bones breaking somewhere in the Canadian's body, perhaps ribs or even the vertebrae of his spine. Then Gastineau gave out a gurgling croak and, suddenly, grew as limp as a rag doll. The big Negro released his hold, and Gastineau dropped to the ground, folding up into a motionless heap.

"Is he dead?" asked Gus eagerly.

Slocum bent down and picked up the Colt Navy. The curve of its butt felt good in his hand, and he had a strong urge to use the .36 on the bearded Canadian. But his rational mind managed to override his rage, and he refrained from firing the gun.

Casey crouched next to Gastineau and laid a hand upon his chest. The black man scowled. "The bastard's still alive," he told them in a low voice. "But he won't be waking up anytime soon."

Gus and Casey then turned their eyes to Blake Duboise. Quickly, she grabbed up her shirt and coat, concealing her bare breasts behind the clothing.

"I knew you were a little too prissy for some reason," said Gus.

Blake studied the eyes of the two men. Both the Negro and the elderly prospector showed no sign of menace toward her. Apparently, the fact that she was a woman meant little to them at that moment.

Gus saw a question in Slocum's face and answered it before he could even ask it. "Something woke me up, and I saw Ol' Gastineau here creeping through the cave, heading for the waterfall. I found that mighty peculiar for this time of night, so I woke up Casey and we came to see what was up. Got here just in time, too, I'd say."

"Did he manage to wake up anyone else?" asked Slocum.

"Not that we could tell," said Casey.

The four looked at one another for a long moment. Then Gus grinned. "We've got our chance, don't we?"

"Looks like it," agreed Slocum.

Blake quickly dressed and joined them at the edge of the pool. "But what about the others? We can't just run off and leave them here."

"I'm afraid we have no choice, missy," said Ferguson. "If we're gonna escape, we're gonna have to sneak out. And we sure as hell can't do it if it's fifty of us instead of four."

She considered it for a moment and realized that he was right. "But we can alert the proper authorities once we reach St. Michael and let them know the whereabouts of the other prisoners, can't we? So they can go back after them?"

"Of course," promised the prospector. "We'll surely do that."

That seemed to calm the woman's worries a little. Like the others, she regretted escaping the Glory Hole and leaving the other gold slaves behind.

"Well, if we're going to do this, I suggest we get to it," said Slocum. "The longer we wait, the less chance we have of pulling it off. Remember, we still have to get through the tunnel to the mine shaft. After that, we have to find a way to the ground level."

"We'll cross those bridges when we get to them," said Gus.

Casey Elder reached to the sash of Henri Gastineau's bearskin coat and withdrew a long-bladed skinning knife. He looked as though he were on the verge of putting the knife to deadly use, and the others half-expected him to slit the Canadian's throat with its honed blade. But Elder's anger had abated somewhat. He surprised them all, sliding the knife into his belt for safekeeping. Then he began to rummage through the foreman's pockets.

"What are you looking for?" asked Gus.

The Negro smiled broadly and withdrew his hand from Gastineau's trouser pocket. "These," he said, holding a ring of brass keys between his huge fingers.

A few minutes later, all four had been released from their bonds. Silently, they shackled the unconscious man and gagged him with the bandanna Blake had used to wash with. Then they crossed to the opposite side of the waterfall and made their way cautiously around the wall of the cavern's unoccupied side.

They reached the mouth of the tunnel undetected. Slocum and the others looked back with regret at the slumbering forms of the other prisoners, then started down the connecting tunnel. They walked quietly, the absence of the restricting chains helping their stealth considerably. They passed the remaining debris of the cave-in, and they all remembered the man who should have accompanied them at that moment. It had been Sean O'Brady, along with Slocum, who had first planned the escape they were now attempting. His absence preyed heavily on their minds as they made their way slowly toward the junction of the main shaft.

When they approached the opening of the seventh level, they found the man named Finch on duty. He was sitting in a straight-backed chair, reading a dime novel about Buffalo Bill Cody by the dim glow of a seal-oil lamp.

The four prisoners got within twenty feet of him before he was aware that he was not alone in the tunnel. "Gastineau?" he asked, peering into the gloom. "Is that you?"

When Slocum and the others advanced a few steps closer, Finch knew it was not his boss who approached. Startled, he dropped his book and grabbed up the shotgun that rested across his knees. An instant later, Finch had the hammers cocked and the sawed-off barrels of the twelve-gauge leveled at the four.

"What the hell do you think you're up to?" he asked incredulously. "If you don't want to get yourselves splattered all over the walls of this here tunnel, I suggest you march right back from where you came."

"We can't," said Slocum flatly. He held the Colt Navy in his right hand, aimed from the hip. "We've gone too far to turn back now."

Finch shook his head and grinned. "Then you'll die."

Slocum ached to pull the Colt's trigger and send a single bullet ripping into Finch's heart. But he knew that if he did, the gunshot would alert both the prisoners in the cavern and the guards who slept in the bunkhouse above. For a tense moment, he and Finch faced each other in a Mexican standoff, neither man willing to give an inch.

Then Casey Elder's deep voice whispered in Slocum's ear. "Step aside," he said calmly.

Slocum hesitated, then did as he was told. A second after he stepped to the right, something metallic spun over his shoulder, crossing the fifteen feet of space between them and Finch in the blink of an eye.

Abruptly, Finch's eyes widened and the barrels of the shotgun drooped until the muzzles pointed at the ground. The staghorn haft of the skinning knife protruded from the center of his chest. The blade had entered him with such force that it had pierced his breastbone and impaled his heart, slicing the organ cleanly in half.

Finch began to stagger backward, but Casey reached him before he could fall into the deep shaft of the mine. The Negro slung the shotgun over his shoulder, sat the dead man in his chair, then withdrew the knife from his chest. It popped free with a grating, sucking noise that caused Blake to turn away.

"I knew this was bound to come in handy," he told them. He wiped the bloody blade on the front of Finch's shirt, then returned the knife to his belt.

With that obstacle out of the way, they turned to the next point of concern. The mine shaft yawned empty before them. The platform of the elevator car was nowhere to be seen. Obviously, it rested several levels above them, out of sight.

Slocum stared at the dark opening for a long moment, perplexed. "I don't understand. Gastineau made it down here tonight, but he didn't take the elevator. If he had, we would have heard the winch sending it down. No, he had some other way of getting here."

Gus Ferguson suddenly grinned amid his bushy gray whiskers. "Hand me that lantern there," he said.

When Slocum had handed him the lamp, the prospector leaned precariously into the yawning gullet of the tunnel, holding the light ahead of him.

"Found it," he said.

The others stuck their heads into the shaft and took a look at what the glow of the lantern revealed.

It was a wooden ladder fastened to the far side of the mine shaft with iron anchors, stretching straight up into pitch darkness.

18

"Looks like a long way up," said Casey Elder. He leaned into the tunnel and stared up. "It's gonna be a bitch to climb, especially after we've busted our asses in the Glory Hole all day long."

"I reckon you'd rather give up and go on back to the mine?" asked Gus jokingly.

The Negro shook his massive head. "No sir. I'd climb a ladder clear to the moon and back if it'd get me out of this place."

Slocum looked over at Blake. "What do you think?" he asked her. "Can you make it?"

Blake Duboise studied the seemingly endless shaft of the gold mine. "I guess I don't have any choice but to try, do I?"

"I reckon not," said the Georgian.

"Well, our tongues sure as hell ain't gonna get us nowhere, only our muscles," said Gus. "I suggest we get going."

The shaft was roughly eight feet wide and eight across. Slocum took a deep breath, then leapt across the dark chasm, and grabbed hold of the crude rungs of the ladder. He tugged on several of them, testing to see if they were sturdy enough. The iron anchors in the stone wall held firm.

When Slocum had given the okay, he ascended a few rungs up the ladder, then reached out and helped Blake across. Once the woman had made it, Gus Ferguson and Casey Elder followed. The framework of the ladder creaked slightly beneath the combined weight of the four, but still seemed to be strong enough to support all of them.

Carefully, they began to make their way upward. Once they left the opening of the seventh-level tunnel, the glow of the seal-oil lamp diminished behind them. Soon, they found themselves in pitch darkness.

Also, the warmth generated by the underground spring rapidly disappeared. They had only traveled a couple of levels toward the surface when the shaft of the mine turned as cold as an icebox. Slocum and Elder wore the coats that had been issued to them on the deck of Shanghai Kelly's ship, while Blake and Gus wore the winter garments they had had when they were captured. The four paused long enough to slip their gloves over their hands, then, gritting their teeth against the cold, they continued their vertical journey.

By the time they approached the fourth level, it was apparent that Gus was running out of steam. The elderly man panted and groaned as each foot up the ladder became an act of torture. Finally, he stopped, hanging onto the rungs for dear life. "That's it for me," he gasped. "I can't go any further."

Casey Elder, however, would not accept his defeat. "Climb down onto my back and hang onto my neck. I'll carry you the rest of the way."

"But you can't—" Gus began to protest.

"The hell I can't!" said the black man. "Now, do as I say, old man, before you lose hold and fall to your death."

Carefully, the prospector did as he was told, knowing there was no sense in arguing. Soon, Gus was stretched across Casey's broad back, his skinny arms linked tightly around the neck of the man whose belly he had stitched up only a few short weeks ago.

For what seemed like an eternity, they climbed, taking the shaft one level at a time. The exertion of the climb began to take its toll on them all. Their muscles began to ache, and the pull of gravity seemed to grow stronger, threatening to drag their bodies off the rungs and into the dark belly of the mountain.

Then, just as it seemed that they would never make it to the ground level, the darkness lightened slightly. Strangely enough, Slocum saw a band of light that stretched between the wall of the shaft and a patch of darkness. He lifted his arm and, surprisingly enough, felt the underside of the wooden freight elevator directly overhead. The light was the glow of a lamp coming from the mouth of the ground-level tunnel.

"Stay here for a moment," he whispered to the others. Then, cautiously, he squeezed through the space between the platform and the stone wall, and peeked over the lip of the tunnel floor.

Sitting on a stool near the elevator winch was an Eskimo guard with a Winchester rifle lying across his lap. From the harsh tone of his breathing, Slocum could tell that the man was sleeping on the job.

Silently, he pulled himself over the edge and stood there in the tunnel, no more than six feet from the slumbering guard. Slocum shook his head in amazement and drew the Colt Navy from his waistband. This is almost too easy, he thought. Then he swung the barrel of the pistol downward, striking the Eskimo forcefully across the top of the head and knocking him out cold.

"We're in the clear," Slocum quietly called down to the others. A minute later, they, too, were in the tunnel. Slocum slung the Eskimo's rifle over his shoulder, while Blake took a .44 Starr revolver from the sash of her moose-skin coat.

"Do you know how to handle one of them things, missy?" Gus asked her.

Blake smiled slightly. "My brother was a seasoned law officer and a damned good shot with any type of firearm. You could say that I was taught by one of the best, so don't worry about me if there's trouble. I'll do just fine."

Slocum watched as she checked the loads in the Starr, then stuck the revolver in the side pocket of her coat. Again, he couldn't help but admire the woman's spunk.

Gus and Casey searched through the Eskimo's pockets, helping themselves to his belongings. Among them, Gus found a .41 derringer and a tarnished pocket watch that had obviously been taken from one of the prisoners upon their arrival at the mine. Gus flipped open the engraved lid and studied the time in the light of the lantern. "It's half past two o'clock in the morning. We don't have much time left till Kolabuk and the others wake up."

From the far end of the tunnel, Slocum saw the pale gleam of moonlight. "Then let's go. And everyone be as quiet as possible. We don't want to give ourselves away, not when we're this blasted close."

Together, the four walked down the tunnel, leaving the main shaft of the gold mine behind. Within minutes, they had reached their destination—the timbered portal that led to the outside world.

Almost dazed by the brilliance of the moonlight upon stark, white snow, they squinted, allowing their eyes to grow accustomed to the glow. "Don't look directly at it just yet," warned Gus. "Moonlight can strike you snow-blind just as easily as pure sunshine."

After a few moments, Gus deemed it safe to continue. They made their way silently past the covered bins of mined gold, then crossed to the rear of the bunkhouse.

Slocum peeked through the frost-coated panes of a window. Stretched out on nine of the room's twelve bunks were Kolabuk and the rest of Arthur King's hired hands. Slocum had a sudden urge to burst in on them, gun blazing, and pick off as many as he cold. But he abandoned the idea. The odds were stacked against them already. There was no need to buck them any more than they had to.

They circled the bunkhouse and made their way toward the dog kennel and the supply shack that stood next to it. But, as they approached the pen, a couple of the huskies caught their scent. The dogs leapt to their feet, growling deep down in their throats and preparing to launch into a fit of loud barking.

Slocum knew that if the dogs alerted Kolabuk and his men, their chance for escape would be lost. "Let me try something," he said. Then, brashly, he left the cover of the boulder he was crouched behind and walked straight toward the kennel.

"He's crazy!" whispered Blake, unable to believe her eyes.

Casey Elder grinned. "No, he's not. Watch."

Blake and Gus both expected the dogs to begin to bark and howl at Slocum's approach. Instead, they did just the opposite. As the Southerner knelt next to the kennel door, the sled dogs whimpered softly, nuzzling at him through the icy links of the chicken-wire fence. Some of them remembered him from having shared the harness of Henri Gastineau's sled during the three days before they reached the settlement of Nulato. The others, in turn, found no threat in the man, who displayed the same calm friendliness shown by their brethren.

When Slocum sensed that there was no danger, he motioned for the others to join him. A moment later, they were at the pen. Miraculously, the dogs showed the same passivity toward them as they did toward Slocum. The Southerner wondered if, in some way, the dogs viewed them as kindred spirits, prisoners of King's cronies, the same as they were.

Gus and Casey went to work. The two handpicked a dozen dogs from the kennel and began to harness them to the front of two sleds, which were parked along with several others beneath a canvas-draped lean-to. While Gus fastened the buckles of the leather straps and secured the leads to the front of each sled, Casey concentrated on the sleds that would likely be sent to pursue them. Taking the skinner from his belt, he slashed the spare harnesses that hung along the wall of the supply shed, then sabotaged the sleds themselves, cutting the leather thongs that held the frame and runners together. After that, he took four pairs of snowshoes and joined Gus at the two sleds he was busily preparing.

Meanwhile, Slocum and Blake were at work in the supply shed, gathering provisions for the long trip across the tundra. They carried armloads of food and blankets to the sleds, along with a few spare rifles and boxes of cartridges for each. The last thing that Slocum toted from the shed was a single crate about the size of a bread box.

"What is that?" asked Gus curiously.

"The downfall of Arthur King" was all that Slocum would say as he lashed the crate to one of the dog sleds.

They finished loading the sleds and tying the supplies down, then strapped the snowshoes to their feet. Afterward, they stood in the quiet of early morning, amazed at the ease with which they had orchestrated their escape from the Glory Hole.

"I can't believe it went so smoothly," said Blake Duboise.

"We ain't in St. Michael yet, missy," said Gus. "We might have a good two or three hours head start. Then

Kolabuk and the others are bound to get wind of what happened. When they find out what happened to Gastineau and the two guards, they'll be after us quicker than a pack of redbone hounds on the trail of a *crippled coon*."

"But they'll have to repair their sleds and harnesses first," replied Casey with a sly smile. "That ought to add an hour or two to our advantage."

"Still, I suggest we head out now and try to put as many miles between us and them before they wake up," said Slocum.

The others agreed. Without further delay, Slocum and Elder commandeered the sleds, while Gus and Blake rode amid the supplies, bundled in woolen blankets.

As they quietly urged the teams forward, sending them down the steep slope of the mountain to the pass below, the faces of all four were grim rather than ecstatic. They realized how very lucky they had been during their escape from the Glory Hole. But they were also aware of what lay ahead of them: three hundred and fifty miles of frozen wilderness that had claimed the lives of many a man in its icy and unmerciful grasp.

19

As it turned out, the lucky streak that Slocum and the others had been blessed with during their escape from the Glory Hole seemed to continue unchallenged . . . at least for the better part of a week.

Following an almost maze-like route of passes, they traveled through the northern mountains as swiftly as the dogs could take them. Several days later, they reached the open plains south of the range. The snowscape was breathtakingly beautiful with its stands of blue spruce and pine, along with frozen ponds and waterways that resembled frosted mirrors set in the snowy earth. But none of them had time to enjoy the wonders of the Alaskan terrain. The threat of capture hung too heavily in their minds.

As they traveled farther southward, Slocum noticed something different about the landscape and the Alaskan weather in general. The snowdrifts were less deep and treacherous than they had been before, and the temperature wasn't nearly as frigid as he remembered it being a couple of months ago. Gus explained that this was due to the coming of spring. It was mid-March now, and by April, the temperature would show a definite rise, gradually melting away much of the snow that lay upon the lowlands, and unthawing the frozen Koyukuk and Yukon rivers.

For a while, it almost seemed as if they had escaped their underground prison unscathed. As they traveled along the winding channel of the Koyukuk, there was no indication that they were even being pursued. Before long, they began to think that they had eluded Kolabuk and the rest of King's men entirely. Gus Ferguson's claim of knowing the land had been no idle boast. The elderly prospector guided them, first through the treacherous snow-laden passes of the northern mountains, then across the broad valleys that lay to the south. By Slocum's estimation, they were less than eighty miles from the settlement of Nulato and would hopefully arrive there within the next week, if their progress advanced at the rate it had since leaving the Glory Hole.

It was during an early morning on the tenth day of their journey that they realized that all was not well. The four awoke from where they had spent the night camped in a scraggy stand of aspen trees, the restlessness of the dogs letting them know that something was amiss.

At first, Slocum couldn't tell what was wrong. He drew his Colt Navy from beneath his coat and, like the others, surveyed the forest around them. But after a thorough search, they could find no sign of anyone other than themselves there. The aspen grove was as silent as a cathedral. Except for them and the dog teams, it seemed that there was no one else present.

"What is it?" he asked Gus. "What has the dogs so spooked?"

Gus flung his blankets aside and stood up. He turned toward the north, tilted his head back, and sniffed the air. "Wood smoke," he said after a moment. "Faint, but it's there. I'd say someone's got a good-sized cookfire going about five miles to the north, maybe even less."

Casey seemed a little skeptical. "And I suppose you can tell what they're having for breakfast, too?"

Gus gave the Negro a sour look, then turned his attention back toward the north. "There's only one way to find out for sure. There's a ridge a couple hundred yards to the west. I'm thinking you could see pert near anything from the top of it."

"Then let's go take a look," said Slocum.

Gus and Slocum donned their snowshoes, then, leaving Casey and Blake at the camp, made their way up the face of the snowy ridge. Once they had reached the top, they studied the terrain that lay to the north. At first, they saw nothing. Then Gus leveled a bony finger toward a dense stand of pine five miles away. "Right there," he said. "Do you see it?"

Slocum shaded his eyes with his hand, amazed at how keen the old man's eyesight was for someone his age. After a moment, he spotted it—a thin column of smoke so faint that it was nearly invisible to the naked eye. He breathed in deeply and this time, caught the distinctive tang of wood smoke in the air.

"Do you think it's Kolabuk and the others?" asked Slocum.

"More than likely," Gus replied. "I'm just wondering if Gastineau is among them. He was broken up when we left the Glory Hole, but he was still breathing. Now I kind of wish that we'd finished off the bastard when we had the chance to."

Slocum knew Gus was right, even though he wasn't the sort of man who held with killing an unconscious man. The Southerner believed in giving a man a fighting chance . . . although, in Gastineau's case, he might have been willing to make an exception.

"What do you think, Gus?" Slocum asked. "Should we head out or stay put and face them down?"

Gus considered it for a moment. "I'd say there's likely eight or nine men in that hunting party down below. That means they would outnumber us two to one. Our best bet

would be to try and outrun them . . . put as much distance
between us and them as possible. Lord knows I don't
normally back down from trouble, and I know you're the
same kind of man, but we do have Blake to think of."

Slocum nodded. Although the feisty brunette had certainly held her own during their trek across the wilderness,
he and the other two men had still watched over her, the
way men normally did when a woman was present. Slocum
could imagine what would become of Blake if King's men
got ahold of her, and he vowed that he would do everything
in his power to prevent her capture, even if it meant fleeing
instead of fighting.

"We'll choke down a cold breakfast, feed the dogs some
jerky, then head out," suggested the prospector. "If we can
keep the distance between us and them the same, we'll be
all right. But if we lose ground, then we'll have no choice
but to turn and take on as many of the sons of bitches as
we possibly can."

"Then that's just what we'll have to do," agreed John
Slocum. The Colt Navy in his belt and the Winchester
44–40 slung across his back didn't seem like much against
a posse of bloodthirsty men, but he knew they would have
to do.

Several days after their discovery from the top of the ridge,
tragedy struck . . . but not at the hands of their pursuers.

It was late evening. The gray light of the winter day
was darkening into dusk, yet they were still on the move,
refusing to stop and set up camp until night had set in more
completely. The gap of distance between them and King's
men had lessened, little by little, until only two or three
miles separated them. If they did not drive onward at a
steady pace, the chance of their enemies overtaking them
would grow greater with each passing day.

They were traveling through a dense forest of thick fur trees, Slocum's sled in the lead and Elder's following closely behind, when a sudden flurry of motion flashed from the thicket to their right. Before Slocum could slow the team, a wolf leapt from out of the woods, landing on the back of the lead dog. The beast was emaciated, the serrated edges of its rib cage showing clearly through its sides. Hungrily, it clung to the flailing back of the huskie, snarling and biting at the back of its neck, drawing blood.

As the sled eased to a halt, Slocum stepped from the back, startled at the unexpected attack. He unslung the Winchester and levered a cartridge into the breech, then walked a few paces forward and fired from the shoulder. The slug tunneled through the back of the wolf's head with an explosion of blood and brain matter. The animal rolled off the back of the lead dog, dead before it hit the ground. But its attack had been a fatal one, nevertheless. Death claimed the lead dog a moment later, sapping its breath until it, too, lay still.

The echo of the gunshot had scarcely died, when all hell broke loose. Up ahead, Slocum spotted the fleeting forms of more wolves darting among the thick furs. He was about to lift his rifle again, when a scream came from behind him. At first he thought it had come from Blake, but no, it was harsher and more manly. Slocum whirled swiftly, but was an instant too late in acting.

A huge timber wolf was perched on the canvas-bound bundle of the dog sled. Slocum and Casey had switched up passengers that morning, and Gus Ferguson rode amid the supplies of Slocum's sled. The wolf had ahold of the elderly prospector, its slavering fangs burrowed deeply into the column of his skinny throat. Past the wolf's head, Slocum could see Gus's face, wide-eyed and drained of color. The old man's eyes were full of shock and mounting agony.

Not wanting to hit Gus with a misplaced shot, Slocum grabbed his rifle by the barrel and, with a hoarse yell, struck the wolf across the side of the head. Stunned, it rolled off the sled, taking a ragged piece of Ferguson's throat with it. As it fought to get back up, Slocum drew the Colt Navy from his belt and put a single bullet between the wolf's ravenous eyes.

Another flash of gray fur and fangs came from the left of Elder's sled. Slocum turned his head and, for a moment, was afraid that Blake would suffer the same fate that Gus had. But before the wolf could reach her, a thunderous boom sounded. Both barrels of Casey's sawed-off shotgun belched smoke and buckshot, engulfing the beast in a hail of double-aught pellets and flinging its torn body back into the forest.

As more of the hungry pack appeared out of nowhere, Casey and Slocum stood their ground, picking off as many as they could. Blake Duboise did not sit by idly while the men defended the sleds. She climbed from the bundle of blankets and, drawing the Starr revolver from her coat pocket, dispatched a couple of the wolves herself. Slocum was surprised—but pleased—by the sureness of the woman's aim. Her shots were not haphazard ones. The .44 slugs found heart and brain, dropping the beasts in their tracks.

After eight of the wolves had fallen, the remainder of the hungry pack decided that their chosen prey wasn't worth the trouble. They scattered, fleeing into the deepening shadows of the forest.

When Slocum, Casey, and Blake gathered around Slocum's sled, they found that Gus was still alive, if barely so. Tenderly, they took the old man and laid him on the snowy ground. Blood jetted from the side of his neck, where the wolf had torn open his jugular vein. Slocum pressed the palm of his hand against the ugly wound, but he knew the act was pointless. Gus was dying. He could tell that by the glazed look in the old man's eyes.

"Listen to me," pleaded Gus, his voice little more than a bubbling croak. "All of you."

Knowing that there was no time to waste, they gathered closer.

"I'm dead and we all know it," he said feebly. "So don't go fussing over my body or trying to give me a decent burial. There ain't no time for that. Kolabuk and the others have probably already heard the gunshots and are on their way to investigate. What you have to do is drive them dogs as hard as you can and try to make up for lost time. You're only a couple days away from Nulato. Head southwest along the Koyukuk and it'll take you straight there."

Gus's face grew so white that it rivaled the snow in paleness. From the slowing of his blood flow, they knew that the old man had just about bled himself dry. As his eyes stared blindly up at those around him, his voice was scarcely a whisper. "John," he called. "Come closer."

Slocum took the man's gloved hand, feeling little warmth through the heavy leather. "I'm here, Gus."

When the prospector spoke again, Slocum had to press his ear to the old man's lips before he could understand what he was saying. "Listen for the crack," he said. "It'll make the trip easier after that."

Then, having spoken that last, cryptic message, Gus Ferguson gave up the ghost and lay eternally still.

With tears in her eyes, Blake Duboise knelt next to the elderly man. She kissed him gently on the wrinkled dome of his forehead, silently mouthed a word of prayer, then took the pocket watch and .41 derringer from his coat pocket, knowing there was no need to leave them with him.

Casey Elder also knelt, a painful sadness showing in his dark eyes. "Good-bye, old-timer," he said. "See you on the road to Glory."

After everyone had paid his or her respects, they knew that it was time to move on. Even as they stood there, they could hear the faint baying of sled dogs echoing from several miles to the north. Slocum and Elder hid Gus's body behind the swell of a snowdrift, then the Georgian walked to the front of his sled. Borrowing the skinning knife from Casey, he cut the lead dog loose from the harness and dragged it out of the way.

When they returned to their places at the sleds, the going was slow at first. Slocum's team in particular seemed lost without the benefit of a leader. But a few urging yells from Slocum taught the foremost dog that he had inherited the responsibility left by his fallen brother. Soon, they were on their way, heading out of the woods and starting south-westward toward the Koyukuk River.

20

They reached the settlement of Nulato at the hour of noon, two days after the wolf attack in the forest and the tragic death of Gus Ferguson.

Time had moved swiftly during their mad dash along the Koyukuk River. They had scarcely had time to eat or rest, in fear of being overtaken by those who followed. And they had good reason for such concern. Their pursuers had heard the shots fired against the wolves and picked up their pace considerably, closing the gap at a rate of two miles per day. Slocum had an idea how they had managed to increase their speed. Apparently, they had done away with one or two of their sleds, increasing the number of dogs per team from the customary six to eight or nine, nearly doubling the huskies' running power.

Slocum, Blake, and Casey could hear the baying of dogs echoing distantly behind them as they arrived at the settlement. They had heard their pursuers the day before, but not as clearly as they had during the past few hours. Along with the barking, they could detect the brittle crack of whips and the yells of men, urging the dog teams onward.

After passing the cluster of primitive hovels and its wooden totem, Slocum and Casey drove their teams in front of Boyd's Trading Post, then steered them around to the rear of the log building. When they came to a halt behind the adjoining stable, Casey turned to the tall

Georgian. "They're getting closer," he said. "They'll likely be here within the hour."

Slocum nodded. He considered their predicament at that moment. The dogs were near exhaustion, and their supplies had dwindled down to almost nothing. He could see no other course of action but to stop running and make a stand.

"Are you ready to fight?" Slocum asked the big Negro.

Casey smiled wearily. "Do we have any other choice?"

"Afraid not."

"Then I say let's take the bastards on," said Casey. "I'm sick and tired of trying to dodge them."

"So am I," replied the Southerner. He helped Blake from the sled as she climbed out of the nest of blankets. "I'd rather you hide in that stand of pines over yonder and let us handle this."

Blake stared at Slocum as if he were crazy. "You've got another think coming if you think I'm going to sit this out and let you two have all the fun. I've got as much of a bone to pick with them as you do."

Slocum and Casey looked at each other, knowing it was futile to try and reason with her. Besides, Blake had already proven her mettle, both in the Glory Hole and in the icy wilderness they had just traveled. And they could certainly use another gun when the shooting started.

"See to the dogs," Slocum told Casey. "We'll go in and see about rustling up some grub." He could smell the rich scent of ham and beans drifting from inside the trading post.

As Elder attended to the teams, Slocum and Blake walked around the side of the log structure, heading for the front entrance. They paused long enough to listen for a moment. The faint baying of dogs sounded closer, but they were still a good half hour away.

When Slocum stepped inside, he was relieved to find the place empty. Only the proprietor, Monty Boyd, and his

Eskimo squaw occupied the building. Boyd stood behind the crude bar, while his wife bent over the cookstove, stirring the kettle of ham and beans with a wooden spoon.

"Howdy!" called Boyd in greeting. His smile was broad and full of welcome, but his eyes held more than a little suspicion. He watched them as they approached the bar. "Can I help you gents?"

"Just whiskey and some of those beans," said Slocum. He had the brim of his hat pulled low over his eyes, on the chance that Boyd might recognize him from his visit a couple of months ago. But on reflection, he realized there was little chance of that. After all, there had been quite a few prisoners, and the barkeep had seemed more interest in drinking and trading with his pal Gastineau than anything else that day.

Boyd set a gallon jug of hoochinoo on the bar. Slocum uncorked the flask and took a swallow. He almost choked on the home-brewed liquor, not because it was particularly potent, but because he hadn't had a drink of whiskey since he left San Francisco . . . and that was a long time for John Slocum.

Before the Georgian knew it, Blake had grabbed the jug and raised it to her mouth. He expected her to sputter and gag on the crude spirits, but, surprisingly enough, she didn't. She downed the rotgut boldly, as if it were no stronger than well water.

"Just the two of you?" asked Boyd curiously.

Slocum studied the overweight man with the handlebar mustache. Stuck in the waistband of his britches was McCoy's Remington revolver, which Gastineau had traded for a fresh dog. "No," he answered. "We've got another out back, tending to the dogs."

As the Eskimo woman prepared three bowls of steaming beans, Monty Boyd continued his interrogation. "Which direction did you fellas just come from?"

"North," said Slocum, feeling that the man's suspicion was reaching a crucial point.

He was right in his assumption. Boyd's expression darkened a little. "But there ain't nothing north of here," he said flatly. "Just empty mountains."

Slocum noticed that Boyd's right hand was resting on the edge of the bar, only a few inches from the Remington. Slocum's own Colt Navy was beneath the folds of his open coat. He knew he would have difficulty reaching his own gun if Boyd decided to make a move.

As it turned out, the move came much sooner than he expected. The door opened and in walked Casey Elder. The barkeep's eyes widened, and Slocum knew that out of all the men Gastineau had brought into the trading post, Elder was the one who had left the strongest impression.

"You!" he bellowed, grabbing for the curved butt of the Remington.

Slocum went for his own gun, knowing that he would never reach it in time to prevent Boyd from getting off at least one shot.

But before Boyd could even draw his gun, he found the muzzle of a Starr .44 pressed firmly against his hairy nostrils. "You've got a mighty big nose, Boyd," said Blake Duboise, cocking her piece. "But I doubt that it's strong enough to stop a bullet."

Monty Boyd swallowed dryly and said nothing. He slowly moved his hand away from the gun and grew stone still.

Blake glanced over at Slocum and Elder. Both could only stare at her in wonder. "Well, don't just stand there. Grab a rope and tie him up."

After their initial surprise had faded, they went to work. Slocum took the Remington from Boyd's waistband and held it on the barkeep, while Casey Elder took a coil of sturdy hemp from the wall of the trading post and bound the man hand and foot. After they had gagged Boyd with a dirty bar rag, they tossed him into a storage room.

Slocum turned toward Boyd's wife. The Eskimo woman cowered next to the potbelly stove, her spoon shaking nervously in her brown hand. "Get on out of here," said the Georgian, motioning toward the back door with his gun. "There's going to be trouble, and I don't want you in the way."

The woman didn't have to be told twice. She flung her spoon into the bean pot and left the trading post and her less-than-beloved husband behind. Through a side window of the building, they could see her heading toward the humble dwellings of the Eskimo village at a dead run.

With Boyd and his wife out of the picture, they breathed a little easier, although the threat of their pursuers still loomed over them. Slocum checked his pistols and Winchester, while Casey went to an ammunition shelf in the trading post and began to fill his pockets with twelve-gauge shells. Blake finished spooning ham and beans into the bowls, then set the food on one of the drinking tables, along with the jug of hooch.

Silently, they sat and wolfed the grub down, chasing it with swallows of the foul-tasting liquor. When they finished, their bellies were full and their nerves fortified. They quietly mapped out what should be done; then, without further delay, they began to make their preparations.

Twenty minutes later, the sound of dogs and men gradually began to grow louder and more distinct. Soon, the party of manhunters could be heard coming through the deserted courtyard of the Eskimo village.

"They're here," said Slocum. He stood directly in front of the bar, facing the entrance of the trading post, the Colt Navy in one hand and the Winchester rifle in the other.

"I hear them," acknowledged Blake Duboise. The woman stood behind a tall shelf in the store side of the building, clutching the 44-caliber Starr in both hands.

Slocum raised his rifle at arm's length and tapped on the raftered ceiling with the muzzle of its barrel. Casey Elder replied with a tap of his own. He, too, saw the approaching party from where he lay on the snowy roof of the trading post. Slocum could picture the big Negro, holding the stock of the shotgun close to his shoulder, his pockets full of double-aught shells.

The Georgian turned his head and stared out the side window. He could see two sleds with long teams of dogs heading through the center of the village, hell-bent on reaching the low, log building of the trading post. Slocum recognized the tall form of Kolabuk at the rear of the foremost sled, but he couldn't quite make out the driver of the second. Following the sleds at an even pace were seven men wearing snowshoes and toting carbine rifles.

"Are you ready?" he asked Blake.

"As ready as I'll ever be," she said.

Slocum nodded. He turned and faced the front door again. He clutched the gunmetal tightly in his work-calloused hands, his fingers lightly caressing the weapons' triggers. He heard a couple of voices yell out, "Whoa!" and then, with a grating of runners against hard-packed snow, he heard the sleds come to a stop directly outside of the trading post.

"Let's go in and see if Boyd's seen any sign of them," roared the rumbling voice of Kolabuk.

"Yes!" came the voice of the second driver. "I want that bastard Slocum and, most of all, the woman and the nigger!"

The familiarity of that voice sent adrenaline shooting through John Slocum's veins. He grinned grimly and waited for the door to open.

When it swung inward, he wasn't at all surprised that Kolabuk was the first to enter, followed closely by Henri Gastineau. The French-Canadian didn't resemble the man Slocum had grown to despise. Gastineau's brawny body was twisted and contorted, as though his back had been broken, and a constant scowl of pain creased his bearded face.

Upon entering the trading post, the eyes of the two looked toward the bar, as if expecting to see their friend Boyd standing there. When they saw Slocum instead, they stopped dead in their tracks. There was an almost endless moment of immobility, as if time itself had been frozen. Then an angry yell mounted in Kolabuk's throat, and he swung his big-bore Sharps downward from where it rested on the crest of his broad shoulder.

Slocum fired first. The Winchester cracked, spouting smoke and flame. The slug hit Kolabuk in the center of the chest, separating his bead-and-bearclaw necklace and opening an ugly red hole in the middle of his buckskin coat. The wound would have felled any other man. But the big Eskimo merely bared his teeth and began to stagger forward, raising the Sharps to his shoulder and thumbing back the beefy hammer of the rifle's receiver.

Again Slocum fired, this time with the Colt Navy. The .36 pistol bucked in his hand, sending its projectile spinning in a cloud of burnt powder. The revolver's bullet hit the Eskimo squarely in the left eye, traveling directly to the man's brain. A puzzled look crossed Kolabuk's savage face, then he fell to the earthen floor with a thud, looking like the giant Goliath slain by the stone of David's sling.

With Kolabuk out of the way, Gastineau was left in the open. He raised a Colt Dragoon at the end of his crooked arm, aiming squarely at Slocum. Before the Georgian could react, a report sounded from just to his right. With a yelp, Gastineau spun and leapt from the doorway, clutching at the bleeding bicep of his left arm. Slocum turned and saw Blake standing there, the .44 Starr smoking in her hands.

From above them came the thunderous booming of Casey's scattergun, followed by the agonized cries of his victims. Rifle shots cracked from ground level, puncturing the building's eaves and shaving off splinters of cedar shingles. Slocum knew that Casey's shotgun would have to be reloaded, so he ran for the front door, intending to dispatch the riflemen before they could pick Casey off the roof. He had gone a couple of feet, when he heard Blake yell out behind him.

"John! The window!"

He whirled just as the glass panes shattered inward. One of King's men stood there, aiming the barrel of a Spencer carbine through the open frame. Slocum dropped his Winchester and used the heel of his hand to fan the hammer of the Colt Navy. Three shots erupted from the revolver in the matter of a split-second. One found the log wall to the right of the window, but the other two hit their intended mark. The slugs caught the man in the shoulder and throat, flinging him backward into the snow.

Blake's gun roared two more times. Slocum turned to find two more men entering the trading post, rifles in hand. The Starr dispatched one of them, knocking him to his knees with a mournful wail. The other, however, kept on coming. His rifle discharged, shattering the jug of hoochinoo on the table next to Slocum. The tall Southerner raised his Colt Navy and, taking careful aim, fired only once. Once was enough. The bullet punched through the bridge of the man's nose, killing him instantly.

Casey's shotgun roared again. Through the empty doorway, Slocum saw an Eskimo guard spin, head over heels, peppered with double-aught buckshot. As he stepped outside, he spotted another man standing to the side of the building, aiming a .50 Hawken at the roof. Before he could set Casey in his sights, Slocum unleashed the last shot of the Navy's cylinder. The slug hit the man in the center of his stomach. He slammed to the ground on his back, the muzzle-loading rifle discharging skyward. Slocum waited for the man to pull a pepperbox pistol that protruded from his belt, but he was too engrossed with the agony in his belly to pay Slocum any further attention.

The Georgian made a quick count of those who had fallen, including those who had suffered from the spreading pellets of Casey's shotgun. Kolabuk and all seven of the others had been taken care of. That left only one to be accounted for.

The brittle crack of a whip and the urgent call of "Mush!" sounded from Slocum's right. He turned and saw one of the dog sleds heading swiftly toward the southwest. Henri Gastineau was clutching at the handlebars of the sled with the hand of his wounded arm, while the other cracked the whip wildly overhead. Slocum knew that if he didn't act soon, the sled would quickly speed out of range.

He stuck the empty Navy pistol in his belt and withdrew the Remington .44 that had once belonged to Tex McCoy. He dropped to one knee, cocked back the hammer, and, steadying his arm with the help of his other hand, aimed down the revolver's long barrel. He found his mark and squeezed the trigger. The big gun bucked in his hand, and at first, he thought he had misplaced his aim. But an instant later, the bullet found its target. A hole blossomed in the joint of Gastineau's left elbow, shattering the bones within. With a yell, the Canadian lost his hold on the sled and fell backward. He landed on his back in the snow, while the dog team continued onward, oblivious of his absence.

Cold rage built in Slocum's soul as he began to walk toward the wounded man. Gastineau sensed that someone was coming for him, and he struggled to get to his feet. His left arm dangled at his side, limp and injured severely in two places. But his right arm was still of good use. He maintained his balance and, seeing Slocum's approach, lifted the Dragoon. He unleashed a single shot, but it fell short of its mark, kicking up snow and earth three feet from Slocum's feet.

Slocum, in turn, didn't miss his aim. He fired again, this time catching Gastineau squarely in the right kneecap. An angry bellow escaped Gastineau, and his leg gave away beneath him. A moment later, he was on both knees, his blood dying the snow around him a hue of stark crimson.

"Drop your gun, Gastineau!" demanded the Georgian.

"To hell with you!" growled the Canadian. He thumbed back the hammer and prepared to fire again.

Slocum's face was a stone mask as he cocked the Remington and snapped off another shot. This time it hit Gastineau in the right shoulder, shattering his collarbone. With a scream, Arthur King's right-hand man slumped forward into the snow. But even with all his injuries, Gastineau refused to relinquish his hold on the revolver. He still clutched it in his fist, attempting to lift it back into line.

A moment later, Slocum faced the man who had made his stay at the Glory Hole such a hellish one. "Recognize this gun?" he asked Gastineau bluntly, his eyes as cold as the winter around them. "Do you remember who it belonged to?"

The rage in the Canadian's face told him that he did, indeed, remember. "Damn you, Slocum!" he growled, lifting the Dragoon inch by torturous inch.

Slocum thought of the way Tex McCoy had died at the hands of the man before him. "No," he said, waiting until the Dragoon was almost pointed straight at him. "Damn *you*, Henri Gastineau." Then he cocked the Remington and fired one last time.

The bullet hit Gastineau in the same place that had brought instant death to the lanky Texan—directly between the eyes. The Canadian stared dumbly at Slocum for a moment, as if unable to believe that he had actually done what he had done. Then he fell facedown into the snow, the hand that held the Colt Dragoon relaxing its grip until the revolver slipped completely from his grasp.

Slocum stood there, the muscles of his arm still thrumming from the concussion of the gunshot. A moment later, he found Casey Elder and Blake Duboise standing next to him. Like himself, both were exhausted, but, luckily, still in one piece.

"So it's over now," said Casey with a sigh.

Slocum's eyes failed to lose their steely anger. "No, not quite. We have one more to deal with before it's through."

Blake nodded grimly. "Arthur King," she said.

Then, together, they turned and started back toward the trading post. With the threat of Gastineau and Kolabuk gone, they would be able to get a good night's rest before they loaded up the sleds and headed out early the next morning.

21

Four days after the confrontation at Boyd's Trading Post, they reached the forks of the Koyukuk and Yukon rivers. As they continued southwestward, Slocum sensed a strangeness about the lonesome stretch of wilderness along the Yukon almost an air of tense expectation. He couldn't understand why such an odd feeling should hover over them. After all, Gastineau and the others who'd pursued them were history now. They had absolutely nothing to concern themselves with in that direction.

As the miles along the frozen Yukon were left behind, Slocum sensed that the weather around them was gradually changing. The icy temperatures of both day and night were not nearly as severe as before, and the snowdrifts along the river grew softer and shallower. Also, they had spotted flocks of geese winging their way northward a sight that would have been unthinkable several months ago.

Three days past the forks, the source of the mysterious tension revealed itself. They had set up camp near a stand of leafless birch, enjoying a meal of jackrabbit, which Slocum had fetched with the help of his Winchester rifle. They were washing the greasy meat down with mugs of scalding black coffee, when a loud crack sounded from the direction of the river.

Casey glanced over at Slocum, a cautious look in his eyes. "Gunshot?"

Slocum consider it for a moment. "No, I don't think so."

Another report echoed from the Yukon. This time there was a brittle, grinding quality to the sound.

"What is that?" asked Blake, setting her coffee cup on the ground at her feet.

Slocum stood up and stared toward the east. A hundred yards away lay the icy vein of the Yukon. As he watched, he detected a shimmer of motion upon its gleaming surface. Something about the movement and the loud cracking that accompanied it awakened a thought in the back of the Georgian's mind. Something that Gus Ferguson had told him, just before he died.

"*Listen for the crack. It'll make the trip easier after that.*"

Suddenly, it came to him. "Untether the dogs," he called to Casey. "We've got to get to the river as soon as we can!"

"But what's happening?" asked Blake.

Slocum smothered the camp fire by kicking a clump of snow over the top of it. "You'll find out once we get there."

A few minutes later, they reached the bank of the Yukon. Slocum's suspicions had been right. The river was beginning to unthaw, and the upper layer of ice was fracturing and splitting apart. Even as they left the dog sleds and watched, the waterway turned into a channel of bobbing ice floes. Then, gradually, the currents began to push the islands downstream.

"So the river is breaking apart," said Blake, unimpressed. "Is that why you wanted to get here in such a hurry?"

"Do you remember what Gus said?" reminded the Georgian.

"Of course!" said Casey Elder. "We can take the river from here on . . . or at least until we reach the point where we can make it to St. Michael on foot."

"Well, if we're going to do it, we'd better do it fast," said Slocum. Casey and Blake looked back at the river. The ice floes were moving faster upon the currents. Soon, they would reach the speed of a dog sled at a full run.

They wasted no more time. Blake gathered blankets and food, while Casey took the skinning knife and cut the harnesses of the two teams, setting the dogs free. Slocum took a coil of sturdy rope from a sled, then opened the small crate that he had stolen from the supply shed outside the Glory Hole. He extracted six of the tubular objects from their packing of dry straw and carefully stuck them in an inner pocket of his woolen coat.

When they had gathered all they would need for their trip downriver, the three stood on the western bank for a moment, searching for the best floe of the bunch. In the back of their minds, they knew exactly how dangerous and foolhardy what they were about to do really was. But they also knew that they couldn't pass up the opportunity to reach civilization twice as fast as they would by dog sled.

"That looks like a good one," pointed out Blake. Slocum and Casey knew she was right. A floe roughly the size of a river barge was approaching from the north, and it was floating conveniently close to the bank they were standing on.

As the floe reached them, they tossed their supplies on the island of ice, then prepared to jump themselves.

"This is going to be tricky, but here goes," said Slocum, then he leapt off the bank and down upon the floe. He land atop its icy surface on the flats of his snowshoes and was immediately followed by Blake Duboise. Both made the jump without any difficulty at all.

It was when Casey Elder attempted to board the floe that disaster struck. His vast weight proved to be his downfall as he landed on the rear edge of the floe. There was a tremendous crack and a fissure formed swiftly, crossing from one side to the other.

As Casey fell to his belly and attempted to crawl to where Slocum and Blake crouched, the crack in the ice grew larger. A moment later, the ice floe separated—just as Casey was directly over the crack. The two sheets of ice swiftly parted, dumping the black man into the frigid waters that raged underneath.

"Casey!" screamed Blake, her lovely face etched in horror.

The Negro went under for a second, then his head and shoulders burst from the churning water. His brawny arms reached out and grabbed the broken edge of the floe that his two companions occupied. But he couldn't maintain his hold for very long. The ice was slick and his fingers began to slip.

Carefully, Slocum approached the edge of the floe. "Give me your hand!" he called. "I'll help you up!"

Desperately, Elder reached out and did as Slocum instructed. But the Southerner's attempt at rescuing the man proved pointless. The more he tugged at the big Negro, the more he lost his footing and began to slide toward the edge himself.

"Let go!" yelled Casey, his teeth chattering from the cold. "I'm too heavy! I'll pull you off with me!"

"No!" Slocum said. "You've come this far. I'll be damned if you won't make it the rest of the way!"

Casey saw the flats of Slocum's snowshoes approaching the jagged edge of the floe and knew that it was only a matter of time before he, too, fell into the icy water.

Slocum felt the black man's huge fingers begin to loosen in his grasp. "Don't do it, Casey!" he urged. "We can make it!"

"No," was all the Negro said before he let go entirely. Slocum attempted to regain his hold, but there was no time. The icy currents grabbed Casey and refused to let go, quickly dragging him under.

"Oh God!" wailed Blake. The woman covered her eyes and turned away.

"Casey!" yelled Slocum, but the man was beyond helping. The Georgian felt a great sorrow overtake him. Casey Elder had saved him from death at the hands of Henri Gastineau, and for that, he was eternally grateful. He just regretted that he hadn't possessed the strength to save Elder from the icy clutches of the Yukon during his moment of need.

Silently, Slocum turned and made his way back to where Blake sat in the center of the ice floe. The woman wept quietly, tears flowing freely through the fingers of her gloves. Slocum spread out some woolen blankets to help insulate them against the cold of the floe underneath. Then, taking the grieving woman in his arms, he cradled her as they continued on downriver, leaving miles of frozen wilderness and the watery grave of Casey Elder far behind.

They rode the ice floe down the river for several days. Needless to say, it was an uncomfortable and nerve-wrenching trip. The comfort of a warm fire was nonexistent; they were forced to eat jerky and cold bread, and the blankets they slept on kept them only warm enough to prevent them from freezing to death.

Also, the floe gradually grew smaller after they first boarded it. The swiftening currents of the Yukon and a few bumps from neighboring floes caused parts of it to crack off and fall away. It gradually changed from the size of a river barge to that of a good-size raft. Slocum knew that a few more collisions could very well condemn them to the same fate as Casey Elder, fracturing the floe into several pieces and spilling them into the raging waters.

They said little to each other during the turbulent journey downriver. A deep depression had gripped Blake, turning her moody and silent. Slocum knew that her mind was occupied with thoughts of those they had left behind, both alive and dead. Slocum also thought of the brave men who had perished: Casey Elder, Gus Ferguson, Sean O'Brady, and, of course, Tex McCoy.

If there was any consolation at all, it was the fact that those who had been responsible for their capture and imprisonment—namely Henri Gastineau and Kolabuk—had paid for the crimes they had committed. The only one who had not accounted for his sins was Arthur King, and Slocum vowed that he, too, would follow his henchmen to the grave.

Near the end of their third day on the river, Slocum knew they were nearing the spot where they would be forced to make their departure, or be swept all the way southward to the open sea.

He thought back to the point of his trip to the Glory Hole, when they had left the tundra east of St. Michael and made the frozen Yukon their route northeastward. It would be at that place where they would have the most luck disembarking. The only problem was getting close enough to the western bank to make it to solid ground safely. During their journey downriver, the ice floe had shifted its position, easing, little by little, toward the center of the river. A good fifty feet lay between them and the riverbank.

Finally, Slocum saw the outcropping of bare rock that marked the crucial spot. He turned to Blake. "Did you ever skip across creek stones when you were a young'un?" he asked.

The woman thought back to the summers she once spent at her grandfather's farm in Ohio. "Yes," she replied.

Slocum stared toward the Yukon's western bank. In the fifty feet in between were three smaller floes traveling at the same rate of speed that they were. "Well, I hate to tell you this, but we're going to have to try it again. But this time it's going to be a lot trickier and a hell of a lot more dangerous."

Blake looked across the expanse of the river. The water that coursed between the floes was terribly swift. She recalled how quickly it had pulled Casey under and shuddered. "I suppose we don't have any other choice," she said.

"I'm afraid not," said Slocum. "That clump of rocks up ahead is where we get off . . . and it's coming up fast."

"Then we had better hurry," she replied, looking a little frightened.

Quickly, Slocum gathered up the blankets, coil of rope, and supplies, and clutched the bundle tightly in his arms. "Follow me closely," he instructed. "And do your best to keep your balance. The ice is slippery."

Carefully, they began to leap from one floe to the next. The first jump was easy. There was only three feet between the two floes, and they made the transition without any difficulty at all. The second was a different story. A good six feet of open water lay between them and the neighboring floe.

Slocum took a running start, then crossed the space to the other side. "Careful now," he called.

Blake followed Slocum's example, taking a few steps back, then running forward. When she had cleared the water, however, her snowshoed feet hit the ice too hard and she lost her balance. Blake found herself on her side, sliding precariously toward the far edge of the ice floe.

Before she even had a chance to cry out, Slocum reached out and grabbed her gloved hand. Soon, he had helped her back to her feet.

Slocum turned from her grateful eyes and gauged the distance between them and the outcropping. The jagged clump of stone was only several hundred yards downstream. If they didn't act quickly, they would be past the point and farther downriver in a matter of minutes.

"Let's try for the next one," said Slocum.

There was only four feet of space between the floe they stood on and the one parallel to them. Hand in hand, they took the leap together and landed safely on the third floe. But they were not out of the woods yet. There was still quite a bit of distance between them and the riverbank. Slocum gauged the stretch of water and guessed it to be a good twenty-five feet or more.

At first, he was at a total loss as to what to do. The distance was much too great to attempt to cross by jumping, and swimming to the bank was out of the question. Even if the currents failed to drag them under, they would end up freezing to death once they emerged from the frigid water. The moment that the cold air hit them, their clothing would turn into garments of solid ice.

Slocum wracked his brain, trying to find a solution. Abruptly, it came to him, although he wasn't at all sure that his plan would be a successful one.

He let go of the bundle of blankets and supplies, then took up the coil of rope. Swiftly, he fashioned a loop in one end, making a crude lasso. After that had been done, he reached beneath his coat and withdrew a knife. It was Kolabuk's ivory-handled Bowie, which Slocum had taken from the Eskimo's body following their violent confrontation at Nulato.

With all the strength he could muster, he drove the big blade of the knife into the very center of the floe, then hammered it into the ice more securely with his foot. After that, he tied the other end of the rope to the handle of the Bowie, much like a chain linked to the end of a ship's anchor.

Blake realized what he was about to attempt. "Will it work?"

"I reckon we'll find out in a minute," he said. Then he took the lasso in hand and waited for the cruical moment.

John Slocum had been a cowpuncher on numerous occasions since he first began roaming the vast territory of the West, and even before that, he had handled cattle and horses on his family's farm in Georgia. Therefore, he possessed some skill with a rope.

He stood on the foremost end of the ice floe and readied himself. Then, as the outcropping loomed near, he spun the lasso overhead and let go. The loop slipped off the pinnacle of rock he had intended to catch, but fortunately caught hold on another that would serve his purpose just as well.

Slocum tugged sharply, tightening the lasso around the stone. Then, as the floe floated past the outcropping, the rope began to grow taut. The Georgian prayed that the Bowie would hold firm and not pull free. Luckily, it remained embedded there. The rope reached its limit, and the floe that was secured to the end of it came to a sudden halt. Slocum and Blake nearly slid of the ice and into the water, but they clung onto the rope and regained their footing.

"Help me!" Slocum called to the woman above the roar of the river.

Together, they took a firm grip on the rope and began to pull the ice floe, foot by foot, toward the riverbank. It was not an easy task, to say the least. The current was strong, and they were fighting against its force. But months of laboring in the Glory Hole had given them the strength and perseverance to tackle such a feat. After a few minutes, they reached the edge of the snowy bank.

They tossed their supplies off, then leapt to solid ground themselves. They were barely in the clear, when a brittle crack sounded behind them. He turned to see that the floe had cracked completely in half, weakened by a fissure made by the blade of the knife. The Bowie and the rope attached to it sprung free as the floe fragmented and continued onward down the mighty Yukon.

"Well, I'll be damned!" said Slocum in amazement. "We actually made it."

"We sure did," said Blake. She smiled happily and gave the Southerner a well-deserved kiss.

Slocum retrieved the Bowie knife and rope from the water, then tied the length of hemp around the bundle of blankets and supplies. He looked toward the west and saw a dense stand of spruce standing a mile away. "I say we camp the night there," he suggested. "Then we'll head out again early tomorrow morning."

"How far until we get to St. Michael?" asked Blake.

Slocum shrugged. "Seventy, maybe eighty miles."

"Without a sled and dogs? Do you think we can make it?"

Slocum smiled. "We've made it this far, haven't we?"

Blake matched the Georgian's optimism. "Yes, we have."

Together, they gathered up their gear and started toward the forest. Both knew that they had to make it back to St. Michael—Blake to win back the deed to her father's gold mine, and Slocum to pay back the man named Arthur King for all the misery he had caused and the deaths he had been responsible for, directly or otherwise.

22

"Wake up."

At the sound of the unexpected voice, Selana sat straight up in bed. The Eskimo girl's heart pounded wildly in panic, and at first, she was certain that it was her dastardly husband awakening her in the early hours of the morning, intent on forcing himself upon her. But in the gray light of dawn that shone through the bedroom window, she saw that the man standing over her wasn't King, but a stranger.

Or was he? She stared at his face more closely. Despite the windblown redness of his skin and the bushy black beard that graced his jawline, there was something about his features that was familiar. Hauntingly familiar.

"I know you," she said softly.

"Yes," replied the intruder. "The Blue Orchid."

A pang of guilt shot through the woman as she thought of all the men she had been forced to seduce and betray. She suddenly remembered the man before her, for he had been the only one among her victims that had made her feel like a true woman instead of a whore.

"I do remember you," she said. "John."

"Yes."

She saw the glint of angry determination in his eyes and felt her heart quicken again.

Slocum sensed her fear. "Don't be afraid. I won't harm you. I know what you did in San Francisco wasn't your fault. I know about Kolabuk and how he sold you to King."

Selana's lovely face darkened with a rage of her own.
"My brother? The devil who sold me into slavery? What
has become of the scoundrel?"

"He's dead," said Slocum. "I killed him myself."

If Selana showed any change of emotion, it was from
hatred to satisfaction. "Good riddance!" she said. "He dis-
graced my family and heaped shame upon the heads of my
mother and father. I hope that he burns a thousand times
in hell!"

"Get up, get dressed, and pack yourself a bag," he told
her. "You must leave this house as soon as possible."

Selana searched Slocum's eyes and sensed the true reason for his presence there. Quietly, she got up, dressed
quickly behind a rice paper screen, and then gathered her
things.

When she and Slocum left the bedroom and entered the
upstairs hallway, she found someone else standing there,
holding a .44 pistol. After a moment, she realized that it
wasn't a man, but a woman dressed in men's clothing.

"What about the servants?" Slocum asked in a whisper.

"They've been warned and are already out of the house,"
replied Blake Duboise.

"Good," said Slocum. "That leaves only King to attend
to." He turned to Selana. "Where does he sleep?"

"In the bedroom at the end of the hall," she told him.

Slocum regarded the two women. "I want both of you to
go to the front gate and wait for me there."

"I didn't travel all this way simply to step aside," protested Blake.

"Don't worry. King will get his due, and you'll get
the deed to your father's mine. Please, let me handle this
my way."

Blake seemed unconvinced at first. Then she heard the

distant crow of a rooster echo from the far side of town, and she knew there was no time to argue the point. "All right," she finally said. "But make the bastard pay."

"I will," assured the Georgian. "I promise."

Arthur King woke up with a cold sensation of pressure against his broad forehead. As he opened his eyes, he was shocked to find the muzzle of a Colt Navy pistol pressed firmly between his eyes.

"What is the meaning of this?" he sputtered, staring up at the dark form that stood next to his bed. "Who the hell are you?"

"I'm just one of the many men you sentenced to a living hell," said the intruder. "One who survived to settle the score."

Beads of sweat began to pop out of the Englishman's pores. "I don't understand," he said. "I'm a respectable businessman!"

Slocum laughed coldly. "Yeah, and I'm Sitting Bull." He reached out with his free hand and, grabbing a fistful of King's nightshirt, dragged the man bodily from his brass bed. "First, we're going downstairs to your study and open that big iron safe of yours."

King considered the contents of his strongbox. It held only a few stocks and bonds, as well as several deeds— nothing that was worth the price of his life. "Yes! You can have anything you want. Just spare my life."

"Let's go" was all that Slocum said as he herded the man from the room.

A few minutes later, they were downstairs. Roughly, he pushed the portly man to the floor in front of the iron safe. "Get to opening," he demanded.

Meekly, Arthur King began to work the dial of the combination lock. Soon, the tumblers were disengaged and the door was open.

"Good job," said Slocum. He directed King to move away from the safe and sit in a heavy leather-upholstered chair that sat in the very center of the floor. It wasn't long before Slocum had the fat man trussed up like a calf ready for branding.

"But you said you'd spare my life," King protested gruffly.

"No," said Slocum with a grim smile. "You just assumed that. I never agreed to anything."

The Englisman watched as Slocum rummaged through the contents of the safe. When the Southerner held a scroll of white paper in his hand, King's face reddened and rage filled his piggish eyes. "The Glory Hole! You must be one of the godless riffraff that I sent up north!"

"Yes," agreed Slocum. "But I'm not taking it for myself. This goes to its rightful owner—the daughter of Charles Duboise."

King's anger seemed to burn itself out. In its place flared raw fear.

Slocum stuck the deed into the inner pocket of his woolen coat. The bundle that he had carried there since the beginning of their trip down the Yukon was no longer there. It had departed his coat when he first visited the study, shortly before he went upstairs to fetch Arthur King.

"Have you ever been in a cave-in?" Slocum asked him. "Have you ever had the weight of a mountain come tumbling down on top of your head?"

When King failed to reply, Slocum continued. "Well, there were some men in the Glory Hole who did—damn good men—and they died needlessly because of your greed for gold!"

He returned the Colt revolver to his belt, then walked to

King's desk. From a crystal bowl that sat next to a cigar box of inlaid ivory and ebony wood, he took a single sulfur match.

"What do you intend to do with that?" asked Arthur King, perplexed. Then, for the first time since being bound in the chair, he spotted a long string dangling directly over his head. Or, rather, what he *thought* was a string.

Slowly, he craned his neck and stared up at the brass chandelier that hung from the center of the high plaster ceiling. In mounting horror, he saw that the candles of the fixture's six holders had been replaced by six sticks of pure dynamite. The explosives were linked by a single fuse, which hung downward an inch or two higher than the crown of King's balding head.

"This is preposterous!" muttered the Englishman, his broad face draining of color, until it was as pale as a bed sheet.

"No," corrected Slocum as he lit the lucifer and touched the flame to the end of the fuse. "This is justice."

Then he left the room and closed the door behind him.

Thirty seconds later, he met Blake and Selana at the front gate. Slocum reached into his pocket and withdrew the deed. He handed it to Blake. "There you go, just as promised."

Blake looked uncertain. "But what about King? We didn't hear a gunshot."

Slocum smiled as he escorted the two women through the wrought-iron gate. "Oh, you ought to be hearing something much louder," he told them. "Right about . . . now."

A split-second later, a thunderous explosion rocked through the ground floor of Arthur King's immaculate mansion. Blake and Selana turned to see the downstairs windows burst outward, showering the snowy lawn with glittering fragments of glass. Then the heavy beams that supported the upper floor began to collapse, one after the other. With a deafening roar, tons of brick, morter, and lumber caved inward, turning the evil millionaire's home into his final resting place.

23

Blake Duboise was relaxing and removing her makeup after a performance in one of San Francisco's grandest theater, when there came a knock at her dressing room door.

"Come in," she called.

One of the backstage ushers poked his head in. "Miss Duboise, there is a gentleman outside who wishes to see you."

"Who is it?" she asked.

"He says that he is an old acquaintance of yours," replied the usher. "From Alaska."

Blake was intrigued. "Please, send him in."

A moment later, a tall, clean-shaven man in tie and tails walked in, smiling handsomely. At first, the actress failed to recognize him. Then she realized that the last time she had seen him, he had worn a heavy growth of dark beard, as well as a threadbare coat and work clothes covered with mine dust.

"John Slocum!" she said in delight. "I thought I would never see you again."

The two traded a warm embrace, then Slocum extended a bouquet of red roses toward the woman. "A gift in honor of your performance tonight," he said. "I've never seen the role of Lady Macbeth handled so magnificently."

Blake was impressed. "I had no idea you had an appreciation of Shakespeare, John."

"I'd say there are a lot of things you didn't know about me," replied Slocum.

Blake eyed the dapper Southerner from head to toe. "Apparently."

"So, what's happened since we parted company in St. Michael?" he asked.

Blake sat back down at her dressing table and returned to the task of removing her stage makeup. "After I returned to San Francisco, I contacted some of my late brother's associates at the Pinkerton Agency. Two of them agreed to accompany a rescue party back to the Glory Hole. As it turned out, one of the detectives accepted my offer to manage the mine for me, and most of those who were still imprisoned there agreed to stay on and work, for a fair wage and much better living conditions, of course."

"And has the venture been a success?" asked Slocum.

"Let's just say that the first shipment arrived by steamer only a month ago, and I could very well retire and live comfortably for the rest of my life," she told him. "But, alas, I am an actress at heart. It would take much more than a fortune in gold to pry me away from the stage."

"Whatever became of the Eskimo girl? Selana?"

"The last I heard, she returned to her village on the Tanana River. Hopefully she can put her past with Arthur King behind her and build a life for herself." Blake eyed Slocum curiously. "And you, John? What have you been up to lately?"

Slocum grinned. "Steering clear of shady whorehouses on the wrong side of town, for one thing."

Blake laughed. "A wise decision, if I do say so myself." She finished her work in front of the oval mirror and turned around. Her delicate face seemed much more lovely than it had in Alaska, and her dark brown hair now hung luxuriantly to the tops of her shapely shoulders.

"Tell me, John, do you have plans for tonight?" she asked as she disappeared behind a dressing screen and began to shed her costume.

"No," said the tall Georgian. "Nothing at all."

"Then let me make a suggestion, however bold it might be," she continued. "Why don't we have a late supper at a French restaurant down the street, then you can escort me back to my suite at the hotel I'm staying at."

"And then?" asked Slocum.

"Well, I'm quite certain I can promise you some plush accommodations for the night," she replied, her voice teasingly sensual. "I'm sure that big king-size bed will prove to be much more comfortable than, say, a hard boulder behind some underground waterfall."

Slocum recalled their passionate rendezvous in the belly of the Glory Hole. "I certainly hope so," he said.

As he waited for her to finish dressing, he watched her trim silhouette through the flimsy screen. This night would surely prove to be one to remember. And he hoped that after it was over, the nightmare of his Alaskan adventure would be put behind him once and for all.